By Any Means

A BWWM Surrogacy Romance

A complete story, brought to you by bestselling author Ellie Etienne.

Faith Richards has always lived on her own terms. Unfortunately, that has resulted in her recently being fired from her job. Broke and almost homeless, Faith has to put aside her lazy, abrasive ways and turn to unconventional methods of moneymaking.

Faith's friend Martha runs a business that matches surrogates with potential clients – a service that Faith has scoffed at in the past – and she agrees to sign up to it.

Soon, she's matched with Aaron, a billionaire who is looking to start a family on his own after a series of failed relationships with gold-digging women.

Their relationship doesn't get off to a good start, but once Faith is pregnant, things start to change for the both of them.

Will her growing baby make Faith reexamine her life, or is she destined to stay in the same rut she's created for herself?

Find out in this emotional rollercoaster of a romance by bestselling author Ellie Etienne.

Suitable for over 18s only due to sex scenes between a billionaire father-to-be and his strong, sexy surrogate.

Get Free Romance eBooks!

Hi there. As a special thank you for buying this book, for a limited time I want to send you some great ebooks completely **free of charge** directly to your email! You can get it by going to this page:

www.saucyromancebooks.com/physical

You can see a the cover of these books on the next page:

These ebooks are so exclusive you can't even buy them.
When you download them I'll also send you updates when
new books like this are available.

Again, that link is:

www.saucyromancebooks.com/physical

Contents

Chapter 1

Faith hit the snooze button. Again.

That made it the third time she'd hit the snooze button. It was now 8:45 am. She should've been up at eight, out of the house by 8:30, and at work by nine.

It wasn't like she didn't want to be on time to work. But she'd started reading a book the night before, and she'd kept telling herself that she would go to sleep after just one more chapter. But what's a girl supposed to do when the writer was so entertaining that she ended up turning the page for just one more chapter until she finally finished the whole thing at four in the morning?

Faith needed her eight hours of sleep. She preferred ten, as did most sensible people, in her humble opinion, but she could make do with eight. Under five hours of sleep, though – that was never happening.

Faith had a fairly useless degree in Literature. She had never wanted to teach. She had just liked to read, and she'd taken the chance to read for her degree. Faith might prefer entertaining romances and whodunits, but she did like the classics, too. It was just that she had no patience for literature snobs. She could appreciate light entertainment and deep, soul-stirring writing.

But she hadn't managed to get a job that had anything to do with her degree except for one lucky time that hadn't ended so luckily. She had been the first one in her family to get a college degree, and she had chosen one that didn't make her particularly employable. The one stint she'd had at a publishing house, hadn't ended well, with her being laid off.

She still maintained it had not been her fault. How had she been supposed to know that she was going through a submission from the boss's favorite godson? It had been complete crap, and she had said so. In just so many words, because she didn't believe in mincing any.

Faith had been fired.

In all fairness, that might have had something to do with the fact that she'd been late to work about seven times in that first month, too. Tardiness was Faith's biggest flaw.

They hadn't even given her a good reference. That, in Faith's opinion, had just been needlessly petty. The godson couldn't write. That wasn't her fault. If he'd been even a halfway decent writer, she could've avoided the whole fiasco. It followed that it was his stupid fault.

The upshot of all that was she had had a series of entry-level, dead-end jobs over the last four years or so. She was twenty-six, and all that hope that had come with being the first of her family to get a college degree had leaked away steadily.

The only time she'd even enjoyed herself had been when she was hired as a studio model for a little while. With her dark chocolate skin, eyes the color of good brandy, and excellent bone structure, she was always a pleasure to photograph, or so she'd been told. But she hadn't turned up for shoots on time a few times. Modeling, unlike what people usually believed, was a tough business. It didn't matter how much the camera loved you if you didn't turn up on time.

So she had bounced along, doing everything from stocking shelves to answering phones to being a front desk pretty face, and she had gotten more and more bored with life. Currently, though not for long if she didn't get her ass out of bed and to work, she was employed as receptionist by a dentist.

That probably explained the dream she was having about giant teeth taking over the world, and being attacked by huge drills, all to the background noise of a huge spit-sucker.

The dream did what the alarm couldn't.

Faith woke up with a gasp and sat up in bed, her eyes wide and a bit wild.

She really hated dentists.

Working at a dentist's clinic quite literally gave her nightmares. But she had bills to pay. She had just made rent last month, and her landlord, Jackass John, was looking for an excuse to chuck her out. She really needed to get paid on the dot, or she'd be out of a home on the seventh of the month.

When her breathing leveled out a bit, Faith checked her phone.

The numbers were glowing: 8:48 AM.

"Shit, shit, shit, shit," muttered Faith as she got out of bed.

She had overslept. Again.

Hopping along, opening drawers, not bothering to close them, running to the bathroom and showering while she brushed her teeth, Faith left pandemonium behind her.

Her shirt wasn't ironed. She didn't have time to iron it. A summer dress was, apparently, not professional. Since it was almost winter, she'd freeze her pert ass off, too.

Well, she was already late. It would just take a couple of minutes to iron the shirt, she decided, and pulled the board out.

"Owww, goddamnit!" she howled when she caught her thumb in the folding table, and glared at it as if it had done it deliberately.

It probably had, she thought, sucking on her thumb. Sometimes it felt as if the world had a grudge of some sort against her.

Sighing, she gave up on the ironing and got dressed. Her hair looked like a bird's nest. She tamed it, pulled it into a sleek bun that left her face unframed, and looked for a shoe that seemed to have disappeared.

Wishing she lived closer to the subway, she walked outside, locking the door after her.

"Ms. Richards!"

Great, thought Faith. Jackass John was the last thing she needed at the moment.

"Mr. Nolan, I can't stop, I'm afraid. I'm late for work," she said, trying to brush past the stocky, flabby man with skin the color of drying cement. He really needed a tan, she thought, looking at him distastefully.

"Notice for you," he said, shoving an envelope into her hand.

"What notice?" she asked, annoyed.

Without a reply, he turned around and walked off, giving her an unwelcome view of his ass crack.

Faith shoved the envelope in her bag and walked off to the closest subway station, tugging her coat close around her.

At least it was almost winter, she thought, trying to find a bright side on a gray day. She loved winter, even when it meant dirty snow like it did in Manhattan. When she was in college, she had spent one winter break in Vermont. That had been the best time of her life. She and a few friends had rented a cabin, and she had realized that she was quite good at winter sports. She'd been surprised. She had never really considered herself very athletic.

She stood, swaying, in the train and got off at the right station, at least. Trying to force down the mild resentment rising in her, she walked back above ground and looked around. How the neighborhood could change in just a few stations! Gone were the shabby apartments of what had become her neighborhood in Harlem. Here, everything was shining and sparkling.

Money, she thought, bitterly. If you had it, you could make more. If you didn't have it, you were expected to be an office drone and make it for somebody else.

Why, she fumed, should she spend her days working jobs she hated when she got only a tiny share of the fruits of her labor? Getting anybody to pay a cent over minimum wage was next to impossible. At least, this time, she was working a job where she wouldn't have her hours cut. She wasn't a temp of any sort.

There had been her time as a waitress – oh, sorry, 'in service', she amended to herself sarcastically – that had made her realize that managers would do whatever they could to stiff you on pay. So she had been late a few times. That didn't mean they should just cut her hours, did it? Anybody could be late, once in a while.

Faith brushed away the unpleasant truth that she had been late every single day for the last ten days. Some days, she had only been a few minutes late, and she was reasonably sure that nobody had noticed.

She paused to cross the road and considered, for a moment. That entire train of thought had been bitter and resentful. She used to be different – bright and hopeful. Twenty-six was far too young to be so jaded and cynical.

She had had so much hope when she graduated from college. It had all been chipped away systematically by a string of soul-sucking jobs that had sapped all the interest from her. Now, a job was just what she did to pay the bills, and she didn't see why she should do more than she had to. She had tried to do it right once – at least, apart from the punctuality bit, because that seemed to be something she just couldn't fix – and it hadn't worked for her.

She sighed as she saw the building with the clinic. It was, possibly, the last place on earth where Faith wanted to be, especially since she was half an hour late.

She knew that the first appointment for the day had been for 9:10. That meant that she'd missed two clients.

Faith shrugged. Everybody hated going to the dentist. The clients probably appreciated the reprieve.

But when she got inside, there was somebody already at her desk.

Ah, that cold, sinking feeling in her gut. This was getting all too familiar. She didn't like the job, but damn it, she needed it to pay the bills.

Faith stood there, uncertain of what she was supposed to do.

"Hello, do you have an appointment?" the chirpy, statuesque blonde at the desk – her desk – asked.

"Well, I'm supposed to be doing what you're doing," said Faith, nonplussed.

"Oh… Oh, you're Faith Richards. Please, have a seat. Dr. Michaels will be with you as soon as he has a minute. But he has back-to-back appointments until twelve."

"I know that. I made those appointments," snapped Faith, irritated.

Blonde Big Tits subsided when it was obvious that Faith wasn't interested in her chirpy good nature.

Faith knew what was coming, of course, but she couldn't squash that little smidgeon of hope that it might not be as bad as she thought. Maybe she was going to do shifts. The cut in hours would hurt, but she wouldn't mind afternoon shifts. At least she wouldn't be late anymore.

She probably would be, but one could hope.

As the minutes ticked by, Faith got angry. She was being treated very shabbily now. Just because she'd been late a few days didn't mean that her time wasn't worth anything. The blonde was obviously terrible with kids, which was not a good thing for a dentist's receptionist. Handling terrified kids was the most challenging part of the job.

Faith was excellent at it.

And, thought Faith with some obvious satisfaction, Tommy had an appointment at eleven. Tommy was a ten-year-old little devil who loved sweets, hated brushing, never flossed, and hated the dentist.

His poor, beleaguered mom had said that Faith was the only one who could handle him.

Sure enough, Tommy came in, took one look at the blonde, and shrieked, "Where's Faith! I want Faith!"

Chuckling, Faith called, "I'm over here, Tommy. Come on over here and tell me what's been happening in art class."

Tommy ran over and grabbed her in a hug that showed strength, surprising for a ten year old. The desperation of being dragged to the dentist could give you strength.

"Faith! Why're you over here?"

"I'm taking a break," she lied.

"Where's Dr. Michaels?"

"He's in there, drilling away," said Faith.

"I'm not scared," declared Tommy, though she could see the chin beginning to wobble.

"You know how it goes, Tommy. You go in, you tell him you've been brushing and everything properly, he takes a look, and if he needs to do anything, I'll come in there and tell you a story. And there will be ice cream later, right, Mrs. Williams?"

Tommy's harassed looking mother nodded.

"Yes, ice cream, Tommy. He's been talking about you all day," confided Mrs. Williams.

"Well, I've been looking forward to seeing Tommy all day, too," said Faith, and they launched into a conversation about the latest happenings in WWE. It was Faith's guilty pleasure, and Tommy adored John Cena.

By the time it was Tommy's turn, his chin had stopped wobbling with impending tears and his eyes were dry. He was determined to be brave, like his hero.

When Tommy went in, Faith's nerves came back in full force. She hated the job, but she did love the kids who came in. She was a kindred spirit, honestly, because she still felt like they did when she had to go to the dentist. They seemed to realize that and bond with her.

She felt the world grow bleaker and bleaker as the minutes ticked by after Tommy left, looking forward to his ice cream.

"Dr. Michaels will see you now," said the blonde, who seemed to have turned into an ice queen after seeing her with Tommy. Can't be used to feeling inadequate, thought Faith with just a touch of spite before she told herself to stop it. It wasn't Blonde Big Tits' fault.

Faith took a deep breath and went inside.

Dr. Michaels looked stern. All hope drained away.

"Faith, I'd rather do this without beating around the bush. You have been late every single day for the last week. I told you, repeatedly, that I depend on you to run this clinic smoothly. I gave you adequate warnings. Today was the last straw. I'm afraid I'll have to let you go."

Faith felt as if the air had leaked out of her.

"Dr. Michaels, please..." she tried, one last time.

"Faith, I'm giving you two weeks' severance pay. Believe me, that's generous, under the circumstances. If you need a reference, I'll give you that, as well. But as you can see, I've already hired Cindy. Please make sure you clear out whatever personal belongings you have when you leave. I wish you all the best, Faith. You're an intelligent and resourceful young woman, but I need a dependable office manager."

Faith made another half-hearted attempt to convince him to give her another chance, but the truth was that now that he had mentioned the severance pay, she was feeling a bit better. Two weeks' severance pay wasn't too bad. She could find another job, hopefully something that didn't involve dentists or clinics, in that time.

By the time Faith grabbed her personal effects and left, the gloom had lifted a bit. She would deposit the check right then and she would begin applying to jobs. After updating her resume, writing brilliant cover letters, of course she'd get a job.

Something far more interesting than managing a dentist's appointments and correspondence, anyway. Maybe this was a good thing, she told herself, cheering up considerably.

In fact, decided Faith, she should celebrate being rid of a dead-end job that would've led absolutely nowhere.

Maybe she should call somebody and celebrate that, she thought defiantly. She refused to be cowed by a setback. As she walked into the bank and deposited her check, she felt her spirits rising again.

Maybe a few books would be a great way to spend a chunk of her check. After applying to a few jobs, she could read, and take the time to catch up with friends. She hadn't seen Martha in ages. Faith decided to call and ask her if she wanted to come over for drinks.

No, she should call Martha and ask her if she could go over to Martha's place for drinks. Her apartment wasn't exactly the Ritz, but it was definitely fancier and more comfortable than Jackass John's palace where she was an esteemed and honored guest.

Making up her mind, she fished for her phone in her voluminous bag, and found the envelope instead. It took her a minute to realize what it was and remember the encounter with Jackass John earlier.

Faith ducked into a café and, feeling secure though her situation, in truth, was precarious, ordered a latte with all the works. She could usually eat what she liked and stay fairly slim, though she liked having curves. When she did put on weight, it was usually in all the right places.

As she sipped her decadent drink, texted Martha, and finally got to the envelope, opened it and pulled the notice out. She read it, sitting up straighter with every word.

"The bleeding son of a bitch!" she erupted, startling a young man on his laptop on the table next to hers.

Jackass John had lived up to his name and hiked the rent. How had he known exactly when she'd lost her job? Suddenly, the severance pay didn't seem like much. Two weeks didn't seem like long enough to find a job that could pay the rent. The delicious coffee she'd been enjoying tasted like liquid chalk.

She was well and truly screwed.

Deciding to use the free Wi-Fi now that she'd paid an exorbitant amount for the frivolous coffee, Faith got her phone out and started going through job sites, applying for everything she could find.

Anything that could pay would do, she decided as she applied to a hotel that was looking for maids, a call center that wanted anybody who could keep their patience with annoyed people, every business she could find that was looking for an office manager, even to be a substitute teacher. She had absolutely no experience in teaching, but did that really matter? Subs barely did any teaching anyway.

Faith tried to think of fancier words to describe her previous jobs. Stocking shelves, waitressing, receptionist for a dentist – none of it seemed very impressive.

Maybe she could find something in modeling again, she thought, but she had been a size two when she'd got that gig. Now she was a size six, which was slim, but definitely not model-slim.

An artist's model, she thought. Maybe she could be an artist's model. How the hell did you go about being one? Or a nanny. She liked children, so she wouldn't mind being a nanny.

Though nowadays, people seemed to hire nannies with degrees in child psychology.

Maybe she should look around and see if there were any cafes that needed a waitress.

But all of those would pay minimum wage. Even if she got fifty hours a week, by some miracle, there was no way she could make rent now that the damn bastard had hiked it. How was it that he could even do it? It should be illegal, fumed Faith.

Her phone rang, making her jump.

Martha, she thought with relief. Martha had been talking about starting a business a few months ago when they last met. Maybe Martha could hire her.

"Faith! Hey! How come you want to meet in the middle of the day, out of the blue?"

Faith had forgotten that everybody but her had work.

"Oh, damn. I didn't think of that, actually. Well, the thing is, I got fired, but I got a severance check, so I wanted to celebrate."

"Faith, honestly. I can't think of anybody else in the world who would even consider celebrating getting fired! What're you going to do now?"

Faith shrugged, though Martha couldn't see it. She sounded exasperated.

Martha was as different from Faith as it was possible to be. Martha was dependable, methodical and meticulous, though she didn't have Faith's imagination. She had worked sensible jobs, done very well in university, and had been looking for the right business to invest in and make her fortune. She didn't often talk about it.

Faith knew she was considering a dating website, or something like that. She wasn't too sure what it was. Martha was an excellent coder, and she was dating somebody who was as good as she was, so Faith figured Martha would do well.

"I've been applying to jobs. I'm sitting at a café for Wi-Fi and applying right now, actually. The thing is, that jackass landlord of mine has gone and raised the rent on me. I wish I could get a rent-controlled apartment! Now I need to get a job. Even with the severance pay, I really, really need to get a job. So I guess the celebration is out of the question," Faith said, gloomily.

Martha was silent for a long moment.

"Martha? Hey, you there? Hello?"

"Yes, I'm here. Faith… How badly do you need money?"

Faith bit her lip. Unless she got a decent job soon, she would need money really, really badly.

Especially because she had just remembered an overdue credit card bill that she'd been planning to pay off over the next couple of months.

"Really badly," she admitted.

"I think we need to meet, Faith. I have some news, and I think I have a… fairly unconventional opportunity for you."

Faith had a bad moment.

"That website you were talking about, it's not an escort service, right?"

Martha laughed.

"No, not at all. But… Well, I think we need to talk about this in person. Why don't you come over? We need to talk."

Intrigued, Faith hung up and got up. She'd go and talk to Martha, if only to satisfy her curiosity now. After all, what did she have to lose?

Chapter 2

Aaron Matthews sat in his comfortable but not too comfortable chair, his back to the plane of glass that would've given him a magnificent view of the New York skyline if he'd been inclined to look. Not too long ago, he would have. He would have reveled in the knowledge that he had made it all the way to the top. He would've enjoyed knowing that.

If anybody had told him two decades ago that he'd be where he was right now, he would've believed them because he had planned it from them time he could think. Even when he was nine, he had known that he would do whatever it took to never have to do without, or worse, make do. At thirty, he took everything he had earned as his due. He saw no reason why he shouldn't. He had worked hard for it. He had taken risks and most of them had paid off.

He had everything he had dreamed of having and owning as a young boy being raised by his single mother who had done her best, but had never had enough. Every time he saw the tired, pale face of the young woman who had been beautiful before life wore her down, he had vowed that he would give her everything and more. She would live like a queen as soon as he was old enough to make that happen.

He had judged himself old enough far earlier than most would have. He had got through school quickly, but he'd been working for years by the time he'd done that. At ten, he had started his first business. Aaron still grinned when he thought of that. He had sold knock-off watches, scarves and bags at a street corner, keeping an eye peeled for cops, and he had soon graduated.

The world of big business, he often thought, wasn't much more cut throat than survival in the world he came from. It was beginning to get boring now that he had established himself as one of the richest men in the world, who owned a considerable amount of prime real estate and invested in the most promising of tech companies.

Everything had become far too easy, thought Aaron moodily. Everybody bowed and scraped and sucked up to him because he could do almost anything for them. Never mind that he had worked hard, risked everything, for everything he had now. Never mind that he made a real difference, paying all his employees well, making sure that every company he invested in did the same. He knew that the policies he insisted on implementing, sometimes against the advice of people who believed in profits above all else, made life easier and more productive for all people who worked for him. They all looked at him as if he could wave his hand and make all their problems disappear.

He probably could. But he wasn't in the business of helping people who didn't have the initiative or the inclination to help themselves. He employed people in whom he saw that hunger that was in him. He gave them the challenges they needed to keep them satisfied, and he gave them everything they needed to evoke fierce loyalty among his employees.

He thought of them as his own, and was still extremely involved in the hiring and firing processes. Aaron had a prodigious memory, almost eidetic, even better with names and faces than with numbers, and he did have an incredible affinity for numbers. His employees felt like they were part of an extended family. He made sure of it. It was mostly sincere. He benefited if his employees were happy and content.

But it was more than that. Aaron knew what it was like to grow up with no security, no real assurance that there would be a next meal, or that they wouldn't have to choose between food and heat during the unforgiving winter. When he first set up his company, he had paid his handful of employees as much as he could without going under. His people were the first and most important assets of his empire. Letting them know that he knew that made sure that his companies, and subsidiaries, drew the best and most creative minds, and kept them there.

Aaron often thought his best decision had been to let his best employees strike out on their own when they wanted – usually with Aaron Matthews as their biggest investor, which kept them in the extended family he had created.

Yes, family was important to Aaron. That was why a frown was currently making his handsome face look quite forbidding.

The combination of his great wealth and his good looks – he had no illusions there, either, and knew that his dark hair with hints of red and gray eyes made women sigh – meant that he had no shortage of dates or dalliances.

None of them meant a thing.

Aaron had gone out on five dates in the last two months. That was almost reclusive for somebody like him. The intriguing, strong planes and angles of his strong-jawed, chiseled face darkened into a deeper scowl as he recounted the dates. He had gone on two dates with the gorgeous Isabella, with her pale blonde hair, coltish but sexy body, wide and inviting smile and sparkling blue eyes that promised wit and charm.

There would not be a third. He had learned to recognize the signs that showed him so plainly that the woman he was with was far more interested in his holdings than in him. Oh, Isabella would've been more than happy to have a fling with him if he hadn't been rich and powerful. But her blue-blooded snobbery would never have let her date him, not publicly.

Aaron wouldn't have minded that a few years ago. Hell, he had enjoyed the dark horse reputation he had acquired. The suspicious glances with which the upper crust had reluctantly let him in had amused him. He had had fun with the rebellious socialites who had wanted to shock their conservative families with a wild affair with Aaron Matthews, the self-made man who was, at the end of the day, not good enough.

The day his wealth had put him on the elite billionaires' list, he had been twenty-eight, and that had changed. Suddenly, his humble beginnings were romantic and compelling, not an obstacle. He had found himself being chased by beautiful women who wanted a rich husband, instead of doing the chasing.

His sensuous lips crooked up on one side as he realized that he found being chased by women far more exhausting than being the one who sought the beauties' company.

He had become jaded and cynical. There had been no help for it. When he was twenty-eight, he had been optimistic enough to get engaged. The lovely heiress, Rachel, had seemed to be madly in love with him. But her true colors had come out when she met his mother. Rachel hadn't been able to hide her disdain at where he had come from, not when she was confronted by the proof of it in his mother, a woman who showed the effects of the hard work she had put in for decades.

Aaron had broken the engagement without a second thought. He hadn't turned back. He'd had no regrets.

But now, at thirty, he found himself desperately craving the comfort of his own family – a wife, the soft sweetness of a baby he could hold and love. He had so much to give. What had he built all of it for if not for his children?

Aaron was supposed to go on a date at seven in the evening. It was three, and he was already regretting it. He'd been set up with this young lady by Dave, who had been his friend for a very long time. Dave had known him when he was a much younger man and risking more than he had. Dave had reason to be grateful to Aaron, though Aaron never thought of that. Dave's family's business had been on the verge of collapsing, but Aaron's shrewdness had pulled them out of the hole they'd been in. Now Aaron owned the company, but he didn't interfere. It should've made their friendship difficult, but it didn't. The two men understood each other.

Well, they did on most things. Dave didn't understand why Aaron was no longer happy to date supermodels, actresses and heiresses who were happy to party the night away and asked for little in return. Dave was nonplussed by Aaron's growing desire to settle down and start a family.

Thinking of Dave's shocked face as he told him what he wanted made Aaron grin.

"Aaron, are you crazy, man? All those lovely ladies ready to fall into your arms, and you want to get serious?"

Dave had been aghast at the thought of losing his wing man.

But Aaron needed a family. He needed that warmth.

If he really wanted it, he thought with a resigned sigh, he would need to get used to going on more dates. Somewhere out there, the perfect woman was waiting for him. She would be beautiful, strong, ambitious, warm, loving and sweet. She would love him, and they would make a baby together, whom they'd both adore. His wife would never be satisfied with staying at home, of course. She'd have a real desire to make more of herself. She'd be competitive and tough.

But Aaron was beginning to feel like he would never find that woman. Definitely not among the circles where he met people.

To his mild mortification, he found himself considering signing up with a dating website. Maybe he could use an old photo where he was not recognizable, and not mention the fact that he was rich. He would probably have to change his name, too.

But what was the point of doing it like that? You couldn't start a relationship on a foundation of deception. Honesty was important to Aaron. He was determined to give his future wife that from the very first day.

With a sigh, he sat down and turned back to his laptop. He had far too much work to do before his date with Maria, who was beautiful, but didn't seem to have much going on behind that lovely face and stupendous body. Trust Dave to set him up with somebody like that, thought Aaron, irritated.

Maybe there would be more to it, he thought, and turned off that part of his mind. With the single-minded focus that was one of his greatest strengths, he turned to the report with its staggeringly huge numbers, and tuned the world out. He would see what he would see. Now, the family that he did have needed his attention.

*****

Faith sat in Martha's apartment, her mouth hanging open. She could hardly believe what Martha had just told her.

"Are you kidding me? Martha, this is bloody ridiculous!"

Martha bit back a sigh. She was used to getting that reaction from people who knew what her website and service was all about. But she didn't see why they had to be so shocked.

Surrogate pregnancies had been an accepted phenomenon for many years now. There were laws to make sure that it didn't end in heartache. She believed in her cause, and she knew that what she was doing was a good thing. She made sure that people who really wanted a child but couldn't physically have one could find a surrogate. Her service was restricted to clients and surrogates within the States, which meant that she was helping exploited women in Third World countries who were often used as surrogates without quite so much informed consent.

Besides, she had the perfect algorithm. She matched couples who wanted children with women who could donate their eggs, as well, if so required, and made sure that the matches were perfect. Very rarely, she matched single people with potential surrogates, too. But Martha's screening process for that was far more rigorous.

"Faith, look, I'm not saying you have to do this. But you remember how much my older sister wanted to have a baby, but couldn't? Well, that's why I did all of this in the first place. I did it for her. I wrote the algorithm for her. She told a few people in her support group for people struggling with infertility about it, and I helped match them with surrogates, too. It's all legal and above board. You are young, healthy, beautiful, and your family's medical history is ridiculously good. You would be a great donor and surrogate if you wanted to be. My algorithm hasn't failed so far."

"But you're actually suggesting that I get knocked up for money!"

Faith was incredulous.

Martha couldn't quite bite back the sigh this time.

"You don't have to do it. But this is one thing where your last few jobs, and how you were fired, won't matter. All that matters is that you are genetically perfect. Which you are."

"That's cold, Martha," said Faith sulkily.

Martha sat down next to Faith on the couch.

"Sorry, I just get far too much skepticism about this. I really do believe that it's a good thing, you know. And it would give you the money to get back on your feet. Apart from the standard fees, all medical bills will be taken care of, and most surrogates built a good enough relationship with the parents that they get paid very well, quite apart from the fee."

Faith bit her lip. She had nearly done a double take when Martha told her how much she would be paid. It was far more than minimum wage. She would definitely be able to make rent.

Besides, she wouldn't be able to drink or party when she was doing it, so she wouldn't be able to spend that much even if she tried. She wouldn't be able to fit into any of the cute clothes she liked, and most of her maternity clothes and so on would be paid for. She would get an allowance for all that.

Faith shook her head. Was she actually thinking of this seriously? What was wrong with her?

"Martha, I am not going to get pregnant and give up my baby, all for money."

Martha shook her head.

"First, you can't think of it as your baby. You have to find the part of you that wants to help somebody else get their greatest wish, Faith. I know you need the money but this is about far more than just money. You'd be helping somebody find their dream, get so much happiness. Wait, I'll show you some pictures, a few testimonials. You'll see what I mean."

Feeling like she was in a dream, Faith looked at photos of pregnant women who looked happy, couples who looked dazed with delight, babies who looked blissfully unaware of how they'd been conceived.

"So how does this algorithm match surrogates and potential parents?"

Faith heard herself asking the question and was surprised. She was going to dismiss the entire idea. She was, wasn't she?

"Well, you give me all the details required in this form, and you'll be matched against the database of hopeful parents. Some of the information in there might seem odd, but trust me, it's all necessary. My job is to find the perfect match."

"So, got any single men in your database?"

Faith had meant that to be a joke, but Martha nodded seriously.

"A few, not a lot. Matching a surrogate with a single man can be a tricky proposition. They have to convince me completely that they have both the time and the means. Single parenthood is tricky, anyway. A lot of people here are gay couples. Surrogacy is a real gift for them. You wouldn't believe how much they want to be parents, Faith. Look at it this way. You do want to be a mother someday, right?"

Faith was taken aback.

"Well, yeah, sure, but someday is a long way away."

"You're twenty-six, Faith. That biological clock will start ticking soon. This will give you the time to start writing that book you've always said you wanted to write, and it will give you a good financial safety cushion."

That was a good card to play, Faith had to admit. She had, ever since she could remember, wanted to write a book. But when you have to focus on making ends meet with dead-end jobs, writing a book becomes a bit of a pipe dream. That had been an excellent card for Martha to play.

Besides, thought Faith, being pregnant might be fun. Sure, you get the twinges and the cravings, but most women in her family had fairly easy pregnancies. That kind of thing was hereditary, wasn't it? Faith thought she'd read that somewhere.

"You would be giving somebody their greatest hope, if you do this, Faith. It's not an easy thing to do. But it might be a good option for you."

Faith made up her mind.

"No. I'm not going to do it."

Martha's face fell.

"But Faith…"

"No, Martha. I'll find another job. I've updated my resume and I've been applying to lots of places. I'm sure I'll hear back from somebody soon. Now let's just enjoy ourselves and forget about all of this, all right? I don't want to talk about this anymore. I'm not desperate enough to sign up for your surrogacy service."

Martha let it go, but she slipped the literature and the forms into Faith's voluminous bag when Faith wasn't looking. Martha had a feeling that by the time Faith was desperate enough to clean out her bag looking for cash, she might feel a bit more amenable to the idea of being a surrogate.

A week later, Faith was getting desperate. She hadn't got a single interview call. She had applied to everything she could find, but she had only got four rejections to show for it. She hadn't even got rejection emails from the others.

It wouldn't have been all that bad if she hadn't had to spend part of her severance pay on a new computer. Her old piece of crap had broken down on her. To find a job, Faith reasoned, you needed a computer, so it was a necessity.

On the eighth day, she was desperate enough to dig in her bag in the hopes of finding stray dollar bills, as Martha had predicted. She found the surrogacy literature and forms.

Angry, she shoved it away. Martha had planted them in her bag even after she'd told her that she wasn't interested. Wasn't it just like Martha, thought Faith, scowling. She wasn't that desperate yet.

Another day, and she was desperate enough to read all the literature and seriously consider the option. By the tenth day, Faith was going through the forms, checking out more information on the new computer, and looking up Martha's surrogacy service.

By that evening, Faith had cracked. She called Martha.

"I've filled out the forms."

Faith's voice was flat.

"I don't want to push you into it," said Martha.

"You're not. It's the only choice I have left. I need to pay for groceries and the Internet by the end of the month. How soon will I be matched with a potential parent?"

"Very soon, with your profile. Faith, you won't regret this."

Faith hung up, feeling as if she had sold her soul a little bit.

She would, at least, be paid to do nothing, she consoled herself. She just had to be pregnant and she could stay at home. She would only have to worry about giving birth and all that months and months later. It seemed like forever at the moment.

Sighing, she found the form online on Martha's website and filled everything in. As she submitted it, she felt as if she was taking an irrevocable step.

Faith shook herself. That was just fanciful, she could opt out if she wanted to, if she found a job that would pay her something better. Besides, it was almost like a vacation. Half the world's population managed to get pregnant. How difficult could it be if everybody could do it? She would be fine.

She should stock up on books, decided Faith, and was soon browsing whodunnits on Amazon.

*****

Aaron was fed up. The two dates he had spent trying to get to know Maria had told him one thing: there wasn't much to know. She was a good-time girl who liked the idea of having a good time with his money.

Well, he wasn't inclined to oblige her.

Brooding, he scrolled through the website, reading all the information carefully. He'd been told about the service by somebody who thought that he might be interested in acquiring it. But that wasn't the acquisition he had in mind.

Making up his mind, he signed up to Martha's surrogacy service, requesting a personal interview with Martha as soon as possible to expedite proceedings. He was going to have a child without having to deal with vapid, gold-digging dolls.

He was going to use a surrogacy service.

Chapter 3

It took only a week for Martha to decide that she had definitely found a great solution for Faith. She had met Aaron twice. Aaron had really grilled her, but he had signed up for the service. Martha had grilled Aaron, too. She'd decided that he was an excellent candidate to be a single father. He sure had the resources to be a great one.

Martha had begun to get a niggling feeling of what was going to happen. And she was right. Martha ran the program three times, just to be absolutely sure, and her gut was vindicated each time.

Now she just had to let Faith know. So she called her.

Faith was so desperate now that she could taste it. How could she possibly have ended up in such a pathetic state? When she signed up for Martha's surrogate service, she had felt like that was it – she had stooped as low as she possibly could, and she didn't see much conquering at the end of it. But even that, apparently, was turning out to be a bust.

Martha had told her that she had a surplus of potential parents and fewer surrogates, so she should have a match in a few days. Well, it had been a week and she had gotten absolutely nothing. Martha hadn't even taken her call the last time she called.

Admittedly, it had been three in the morning, but a shrewd entrepreneur would be awake and working at that hour, wouldn't they?

When Faith finally got the call, she was ready to weep with relief.

"Martha! I tried calling you."

It came out as a peeved and petulant complaint. Faith couldn't help it.

"Well, I'm calling you back, and I've got news."

"You've matched me with a couple! You've found somebody!"

A few weeks ago, Faith would never have believed that the thought of being a surrogate could give her so much relief and sheer joy.

"Well, yes, but it's a bit unconventional and a bit complicated. Why don't I come by and tell you about it in person?"

Faith looked around her home. Apart from being tiny and nothing much to write home about, it was also incredibly messy at the moment. She compared it unfavorably with Martha's neat and colorful apartment, and decided that there was no way she was inviting Martha over. Neither did she feel like cleaning it up before she got there. What was the point of cleaning it all up when she would only get it all messy again, rationalized Faith as she did quite often.

"Why don't I come over there? I could use some fresh air."

She really could, especially since she'd finished a good part of a bottle of vodka the night before. If it worked out and she did get matched with potential parents, they would probably insist on things like not drinking. If it didn't work out, then she sure had sorrows to drown. Either way, the bottle of vodka had seemed like a great idea the night before.

The splitting headache she had at the moment seemed to prove that it was yet another of her bright ideas that didn't work out too great. She did seem to have a lot of those, thought Faith with a sigh.

"All right, why don't you come on over, then?"

So Faith got her oversized sunglasses on and went out to meet Martha. She didn't know it, but her life was about to change completely.

Faith considered getting a cab over, but her bank balance was beginning to cry really loudly, so she took the subway, getting grumpier all the way.

It wasn't fair, thought Faith. She was considered lazy and unmotivated. But if all that she had to motivate herself was staying in her crappy apartment, why would she do anything more than she had to do? What was the point of it? The rich just got richer, all the time, and everybody else fought for what was left. She hated the ones who fed on self-righteousness.

The hangover was making her extra grumpy and moody. She really didn't like herself when she was like this. Faith tried to shake it off as she walked up to Martha's place.Faith couldn't help the stab of jealousy as she got in the elevator and pressed a number in the double digits. Martha lived in a really nice place. If Faith could just see a real way out, to something more than more of the same, she really would put in the effort. In her life as it was, it just seemed so pointless.

Faith's disposition wasn't improved when Martha opened the door looking so well-groomed that she looked like a drowned rat in comparison.

"Ah, Faith. You're here. You look… well."

The significant pause did not go unnoticed.

"Well, what have you got for me?" asked Faith, trying not to feel too resentful. Or at least, trying not to show the resentment.

"Come in, sit down. You're probably going to like this. It's a bit unusual, but, well, you don't mind the unusual and the unconventional, do you? You never have."

Faith thought something fishy was going on.

"Martha, what the hell is going on?"

"Well, I've found the perfect match for you. But it's a bit complicated."

"Yes, so I gathered. Spill the beans, Martha," said Faith, irritated.

"Well, it's not a family, not the way you think of it. It's a single man. He is an excellent prospect as a father, and he wants to have a child. He can't find the right woman to have the child with, so he signed up with us. Now, you should know that we vet single males very thoroughly, so this is the real deal."

"So he's got a good job and a home and stuff?"

"Well, yes, obviously. Better than that, actually. But he does have a few conditions, and I want to tell you what those are first."

Faith shrugged.

"He's going to have the… the procedure done the scientific way. I'm not sleeping with him to get knocked up."

Martha's mouth fell open in shock.

"Faith… Faith, I would never even consider something like that, you know that!"

Faith shrugged.

"Just sayin'. So what are these conditions?"

"Well, he wants to get to know you first. I haven't sent him your profile yet, but I have complete faith in my algorithm. It'll work out. I'm sure you'll get along, and he'll see that you're the ideal surrogate."

That sounded like a bit of a canned speech to Faith. Something was just a little bit off.

"Martha, what the hell are you talking about? The whole deal is supposed to be that you do the matching. It's not a dating service. Or an escort service. So what's all this about?"

"Well, there are exceptional clients and exceptional circumstances, Faith. This is one of them."

"What's so exceptional about this?"

"All right. This client is Aaron Matthews."

It took Faith a few seconds to compute.

"Aaron Matthews? The billionaire Aaron Matthews? The man who seems to own so much stuff that he'd find it difficult to figure out what he doesn't own? That Aaron Matthews has signed up to your surrogate service? He can't find himself a baby mama?"

It seemed more and more ridiculous as Faith went on.

"Yes, that Aaron Matthews. And this is on the level, Faith. I met him. Boy, he sure grilled me! He wants to have a family, Faith. But he can't find the right woman. Now, I'm not saying you're the right woman for him, but you are the perfect mother for his child."

Faith was silent. She was thinking.

"Aaron Matthews wants me to have his child."

She let out a long whistle.

"Well, well, well. Haven't I hit the jackpot!"

Martha looked uneasy.

"Faith, it isn't like that. I mean, sure, you will be compensated and there will be a bonus depending on the client, but it's not like you'll be set for life thanks to this."

"You said he wants to get to know me first. Isn't your 'highly accurate algorithm' enough for that?"

"Well, he said he trusts himself and his own judgment more than it, so..."

Martha looked and sounded extremely miffed that he wouldn't put all his faith in her algorithm.

Faith shrugged.

"Well, if your algorithm says so, it must be right. Right? So what's he like?"

Martha fidgeted a bit.

"He's... Well, he's very handsome."

Faith rolled her eyes.

"Well, of course he is. We've all seen him in the magazines and the tabloids. What's he like apart from the looks and the money?"

Martha shrugged.

"Driven, ambitious, demanding. I suppose most self-made billionaires are like that."

Faith was cynical about the 'self-made' part of it. As far as she was concerned, the only way anybody became a billionaire was if they started with millions. Nobody was 'self-made', definitely not a billionaire.

Besides, she didn't like driven, demanding men. She liked easygoing, mellow men who were happy to go with the flow, not regimented men who needed to schedule every little moment.

But she could deal with a finicky billionaire if it would set her up for life. She definitely intended to play her cards right. If he was so keen on having a child, he could pay enough to make sure that she was taken care of for a good, long while, decided Faith.

"So, how do we seal the deal?"

Martha looked startled, as if she hadn't expected Faith to get on board quite so quickly.

"Well, he wants to meet you and get to know you," said Martha.

"So… He wants to date me to see if I'm fit to be the mother of his child."

"Not quite. I insisted that he sign up for the service, and sign the contract, if he wants to meet you and spend time with you. You will be compensated even if he changes his mind now. But if you change your mind, there will be a payment to be made, so you have to be sure, Faith," warned Martha.

Faith was sure. After all, when you didn't have options, it was quite easy to be very sure about something that seemed frankly ridiculous.

"I'm sure. Give me the contract and I'll sign it."

Martha looked a bit uneasy now.

"Faith, you should take this seriously. It's a big commitment. You should think about it."

Angry, Faith got up and paced.

"Think about what? That I'm so out of options that I'm willing to sign that contract without even reading the fine print? Believe me, I've thought about it. But this is the only real option I've got. I need to make rent. And I don't want to live from paycheck to paycheck all my life. I want some security. I want to be able to spend money when I want something. Why shouldn't I? I want to have a good time! So I'm just renting my womb out for nine months so that I can have that. If I'm having a billionaire's baby, I can bloody well get a good bonus for it."

Martha was silent. She didn't quite like being faced with her friend's desperation like that.

Then she nodded.

"Fine. The contract is here. He has already signed it. Once you've signed it, I'll give him your phone number. He will call you to set up a meeting. You get to choose when you want the insemination procedure to be, as long as it's within the next six weeks. After that, he will get to see you once a week. He insisted on that, too. You will also be making a commitment that you will eat right, exercise right, and so on. The doctor's bills will be taken care of by him. The first lump sum will be paid to you within the week. The rest will be paid every three months until the due date. He will have the right to make sure that you are taking care of yourself during the pregnancy. Is that all fine with you?"

Faith nodded. She didn't like the idea of some billionaire getting to sign off on her eating, sleeping, and workout habits over the next nine months, but she could deal with it. She needed the money.

Besides, nine months wouldn't be that long. And it wasn't like he could supervise her the entire time.

Maybe he could, but he wouldn't, would he?

She would know when she met him.

Faith signed the contract and left, knowing that she had done something that would affect her for the rest of her life. She hoped she had made the right decision.

But honestly, there hadn't been all that much of a decision to make. It was this or not make rent.

Determined to make the best of it, Faith went back to her apartment and got to work finishing the rest of that bottle of vodka. She'd be giving it up for nine months, at least, unless there was some weird breastfeeding contract. Then it would be for longer. She might as well make the most of the time she had to do whatever she felt like.

*****

Aaron had the contract in front of him. It had been messengered over to him by Martha. He had definitely read every word of it, including the finest of fine print.

He would be committing his money, and nothing more, at this point. He could call off the entire thing as long as he paid the surrogate her fee, and, probably, a good bonus.

He went through the profile of Faith Richards. He didn't really see much that appealed to him. She was beautiful, of course, but he had expected that. Beauty wasn't a prerequisite for him, but he had expected the surrogacy service to assume that it would be. It didn't matter.

He hadn't specified that he wanted a mixed race baby, but now that he thought about it, he decided that their child would be perfect.

Now he just needed to get to know this Faith Richards and find out what she was actually like. After all, it wasn't only physical traits that were hereditary. He needed to know what this woman was really like – what made her tick, what didn't.

Apart from everything else, even if she would be signing over all rights as a parent, he wouldn't be against the idea of having her in the child's life if she wanted something to be worked out that way. But he could only do that if the woman was worthy of being in his child's life.

He would also want to monitor the baby's health, and make sure that everything was fine. He would talk to the best doctors and get the perfect guidelines for her to follow. Everything possible would be done to be sure that the baby was given every chance to develop into a little bundle of perfection.

The thought made him smile, transforming his face as a look of complete tenderness passed over it. There were very few people in the world who would've recognized that look on his face.

Now, he needed to meet Faith Richards, and see how things went. The first meeting, if he so chose, could be with Martha, or without. He was leaning towards meeting Faith at a café, away from supervision or prying eyes. He didn't want her to pretend to be somebody she wasn't.

He kept the pen poised over the contract and took a deep breath. This would change everything about his life. It would give him what he wanted more than anything in the world.

Finally, he was taking a solid step towards having a child – a little person of his own. It might not be the ideal way, but he would have a family.

He signed on the dotted line.

*****

Faith opened a rather bleary eye when the phone rang. At least she couldn't feel a hangover waiting to pounce this time. That was an improvement on the day before. She checked the time – it was 9:30. Now that she was unemployed, that seemed very early to her.

Her phone had beeped because she'd gotten an email. For a moment, she perked up, thinking that she might have finally gotten a reply from one of the places she'd applied to. The hope leaked away as she remembered that it didn't matter anymore. She had signed up to be a surrogate. She had already signed.

It wasn't so bad, she told herself, and checked her email.

Slowly, she sat up and read it again.

Dear Faith,

I'm sure you've been expecting to hear from me. I'm Aaron Matthews. I got your email id and contact number from Martha.

I considered calling you, but I decided that an email would be easier for both of us.

I would like to meet you sometime today, if possible, for a chat. Now that we've both signed the contract, the next logical step is for us to get to know each other. I'm sure this counts as a fairly unusual situation, so I'm not sure how to proceed with this. If there's a café you're comfortable with, I'd be agreeable to meeting you there. However, I'm only free at 2:30 PM, so I hope that works for you.

If we both decide to go forward with it, there are a lot of details to iron out.

I would like to assure you, first and foremost, that if you do change your mind after meeting me, I will still honor the agreement. I believe that's the least I could do under the circumstances.

If you prefer to have our first meeting with Martha, we can do it that way, as well.

Yours sincerely,

Aaron Matthews.

Faith pursed her lips and read it a couple of times.

What was Martha on about? He seemed perfectly nice. A bit still and formal, but that was to be expected. It was… how had he put it? An unusual situation.

So he wanted to meet and make sure she would be good as a baby vessel. She could deal with that. She was free all the time, of course, but she could meet him for coffee.

Faith deliberated her reply for a while, and finally hit send.

Hi Aaron,

I'm very glad to hear from you! Yes, it is an unusual situation, but I'm sure we can make it work to be as comfortable as possible. Martha tells me that you really want to have a child. She's shown me stories of parents who've been helped by surrogates, and I'm inspired. If I can do something similar for you, I'm all for it.

But I do think it would be a smart thing for us to meet and finalize all the details. I've never done this before, so I don't really know what the protocol is! Anyway, I hope that we'll be friends. I do think it's important that I'm friends with the father of the child I will carry and cherish for nine months.

I believe Kaffee und Kuchen is close to your offices. I would be glad to meet you there today at 2:30 PM.

I look forward to a meaningful relationship.

Thanks!

Faith

Faith read it again after she sent it and decided that she'd done about as good a job as possible. It wasn't as stiff and formal as his email. She thought it expressed her more easygoing personality quite well.

So, thought Faith, feeling energized – she would soon be meeting the father of the baby she would probably have.

She would also be meeting her first billionaire. She didn't want to be too cavalier about the whole thing, but she did hope that she would make a good impression. She needed that bonus.

Unsure of what to expect, Faith spent the next few hours choosing and discarding outfits. She rejected multiple combinations for different reasons – too staid, too boring, too interesting, too out there. Finally, she settled on a figure-hugging dress that didn't show too much cleavage or legs. She wouldn't be able to wear stuff like that for a long time if she got pregnant. Once she got pregnant, she corrected herself – she needed to stop thinking of it as an 'if'. She might as well wear it as often as she could before that.

As usual, Faith lost track of time as she did her makeup and her hair. Finally satisfied, she stepped out of the door, locked up and checked the time. She nearly did a double take. She had only about ten minutes! There was absolutely no way she would make it to Kaffee und Kuchen on time.

Well, thought Faith with a shrug, a man could learn to wait for the future mother of his child. Feeling rich, she hailed a cab and settled down, on her way to meet Aaron Matthews, billionaire, to talk to him about the logistics of having his baby.

This, thought Faith, was going to be very interesting.

Chapter 4

Aaron was extremely annoyed. This was off to a bad start and he hadn't even met the woman yet.

She was late. He hated tardiness. It was a sign of complete inefficiency and lack of respect. Did the woman have the slightest idea what his time was worth?

He took his tablet out and got to work. If she didn't care about wasting time, he did. He would get some work done while he waited for Faith Richards.

It was twenty minutes before Faith got there. She got out of the cab, gulping a little at how much cab fare had come to, and added a reckless tip. Faith liked to be generous when she could.

She caught a glimpse of Aaron through the glass window. He looked handsome and rich. Faith grinned. Her star was rising. So what if she had to deal with a pregnancy? She would finally be comfortable! Besides, he was absolutely hot. If she'd met him on an online dating site, or been set up by a friend, she'd totally go for him.

She refused to acknowledge how her heart was thundering, or how her legs felt like they'd suddenly been turned to jelly. She was being silly. There was absolutely no reason to feel like she was making a huge mistake. She had thought this through. Anyway, it wasn't as if she had much of a choice.

"Fake it till you make it," she muttered to herself, and took a deep breath.

There was a swagger in her gait as she walked in and to Aaron's table. She waited for him to notice her.

He didn't notice her.

"Ahem."

Faith cleared her throat theatrically.

Aaron looked up with a frown on his face and recognized her. He didn't get up, but motioned towards the chair opposite him.

Faith was about to speak, but he raised a hand and made a shushing gesture.

Well! Of all the nerve! She had chosen the café for his convenience, hadn't she? She had paid cab fare to get all the way over there, and here he was, acting as if she weren't even there! These rich bastards, thought Faith, fuming, thought they just owned everybody just because they had money.

They probably did own a lot of people. If you owned their debts and their livelihoods, wasn't it as close as you got nowadays to actually owning people?

Seething, Faith waited five whole minutes before he finally deigned to look up and give her some of his precious attention. When he did talk, his voice was as appealing as his looks, but now Faith was pissed off.

"Ms. Richards. I apologize for keeping you waiting, but in all fairness, you kept me waiting a lot longer."

Faith shrugged. She had come in ready to apologize for her tardiness, but his high and mighty behavior wasn't winning her over. He could suck it.

"We have both signed the contract. We can iron out any extra details, if we both decide to go through with this, over the next few months. Could you, perhaps, tell me why you decided to sign up for this service?"

Faith contemplated giving him a canned response, but decided to screw it and give him the truth. He had already said that if he changed his mind, she would still get the money. What did she have to lose now?

"I need the money."

Aaron waited, as if he expected her to elaborate. But what else was there to say? Everybody needed money. She needed it more than anybody he was likely to know, sitting on his bloody throne made of dollar bills.

"All right. You will get the money, obviously. Could you tell me something about yourself?"

"Should've thought of this before you signed the contract, shouldn't you?"

Faith couldn't hide the smirk.

"The money isn't a considerable sum for me."

"Oh yes, you're a billionaire. Well, whoop-di-doo, didn't I hit the jackpot."

Aaron's eyes went hard and cold. Despite herself, Faith felt a thrill run through her body. Damn, but he was hot, especially when he looked as forbidding as that.

"Ms. Richards…"

"Please, call me Faith. If I'm going to have your baby, we should at least be on first name basis, right?"

When she said that, Aaron saw that mask slip for a moment.

Of course, it clicked. This was mostly bravado. It must be a difficult situation for her to be in. He should probably be more approachable and more understanding, decided Aaron, and tried to soften a little.

"Faith, I would like us to be able to get along with each other. If we do this, we're going to be in each other's lives for a few months. Maybe longer. It would be more convenient all around if we could learn to understand each other a bit, wouldn't it?"

Faith sneered at him.

"Really, you think you could understand me? You're rich. You could have whatever you wanted. Probably born with a silver spoon, hell, a whole silver place setting in your mouth. What would you know about having to worry about making ends meet, wondering how you're going to make rent?"

Aaron was taken aback. So she didn't know his background. How odd, he mused. He had got used to snobs not considering him good enough for them. Now apparently he was in the presence of some classic reverse snobbery.

It didn't matter. He had dealt with the one. He could deal with the other.

"I don't need to understand you. You have signed a contract to provide me a service. I have agreed to adequately compensate you for it. We need to sort out the details. I have here a list of clinics that I'd prefer to use. They will take care of the initial procedure, and everything you need until the delivery. Here is some literature for you. These are the guidelines I will expect you to stick to while you're pregnant. Those are non-negotiable. If it's all agreeable to you, we can set up an appointment at the clinic you choose from the list."

Faith was uneasy. This wasn't how she had pictured it at all. She wasn't sure how she had pictured it, really. She'd avoided thinking about it. But whatever she'd expected, it hadn't been this.

"That's a bit cold, isn't it?"

She couldn't quite keep that quaver out of her voice.

"It's a business proposition, Faith. Is there anything you'd like me to know about you?"

She was taken aback. That was an odd question.

"No," said Faith, summoning up every bit of pride she could find.

"Well, then. I'm afraid that's all the time I have today. Here's a check – the first payment. It's quite generous, above and beyond what's dictated in the contract. I trust that it will keep you in comfort until the next payment. You have my email. Here's my phone number. You can call me, or preferably, email me, when you've chosen the clinic. I will give you a date and time that will be suitable for me. I hope you can make that work?"

Faith gawked. She couldn't really trust herself to say anything.

"I think we need to consult my ovaries before you schedule it. Don't I have to be ovulating? Isn't that necessary?"

That made Aaron pause. She liked seeing his smug face get a bit less smug.

"Right. Email me with that and I will set it up. If you'd like me to get in touch with your gynecologist, that can be arranged. I wish you good day, Faith."

With a lissome grace that Faith had to appreciate, stunned as she was, he was up and off, leaving her with a check and a business card.

The damn bastard hadn't even given her cab fare back, thought Faith as she took the check. The number of zeroes on it had her thinking slightly more charitable thoughts about Aaron Matthews.

But the zeroes wouldn't count until she actually deposited the check. With a sigh, she got up and decided she'd better get a subway home. She could stop at a bank before she got on and deposit the check. Then she could live like a queen for a while.

What a stone cold bastard Aaron Matthews was! She should talk to Martha and tell her what she thought of her perfect, highly accurate algorithm. If it thought that she and that rich jackass were a good match for anything, it couldn't possibly be more wrong.

*****

Aaron set Faith out of his mind as he got back to work. He couldn't afford to be distracted. His work was far too important.

But in the background ran the humming sense of dissatisfaction. How could Martha possibly have thought that Faith would be the ideal surrogate for his child? Highly accurate algorithm, bloody buggering horse shit!

Maybe he should just call the whole thing off. Maybe he should call Martha and tell her that he had changed his mind. He could pay the whole fee. Money wasn't a problem.

Faith was tardy, inefficient, arrogant, a snob and had absolutely no respect for him. She had spent the entire time looking down her nose at him, as if he were beneath her. Worse, she had assumed that she had won some kind of lottery – as if she had found herself a never-to-be-depleted personal ATM!

Well, she would soon find out otherwise, wouldn't she!

Impatient, he pushed his work aside and called Martha.

"Aaron, how did the meeting go?"

"You said you know Faith. You tell me how you think the meeting went."

"I did suggest that you have the meeting with me present."

"Does your presence alter the basics of Faith's personality?"

Aaron didn't bother to bite back the sarcasm.

"Look, Faith is in a bit of a trying situation at the moment and that bleeds into her attitude a bit. I've known her a long time. She is a wonderful person. You haven't seen the warm, kind, generous, fun side of her. I'm sure she was on the defensive, and that gave a bad first impression. Please, just give it some time and you'll see that I'm right. Besides, my algorithm..."

"Good Lord, woman, if you mention your algorithm one more time..."

Martha wisely bit her tongue. She needed to call Faith and ask her just what she had done to get him so worked up.

But her doorbell rang right then.

"Martha, I know you're in there! It's me, Faith, open the damn door!"

Martha sighed.

"Aaron, Faith is here. I have to go. I hope you will choose to give this time. I hope that Faith hasn't changed her mind. Please, go through the reports and the profile again. You agreed that, on paper, Faith is perfect. That's what you'll be getting in your child, don't forget that. We could even go the egg donor way if you like, but I really think Faith would be perfect. Think about it and let me know what you decide."

Aaron looked at his phone, speechless, when he realized that Martha had hung up on him. Apparently, it was his day for rude, discourteous women.

Martha opened the door, wincing. She knew what was coming.

"He might be rich, but what a smug, insufferable bastard he is with all his dollars!"

Faith brushed right past her, stalked into the living room and parked herself on the couch. Resigned, Martha settled down to listen to more of the same. According to Faith, Aaron Matthews was everything that was wrong with the world.

But Martha knew Faith. She could see the nerves playing behind all of that outrage. So she let Faith talk it all out and finally asked her what the real problem was.

Faith was quiet for a long moment.

"I'm scared," she admitted, finally.

Martha slipped an arm around her shoulders supportively.

"I know. He called me just now and he picked up on that, too."

"He did?"

"Well… Not really. To anybody who doesn't know you, it comes across more as belligerence than fear and uncertainty, Faith. But think of it this way. He's making a life-changing decision, too. If you're scared, well, he probably is, too. I don't think you saw the best of each other. So go home, get some sleep, and think about it."

"He calls the shots now," mumbled Faith.

Martha sighed.

"He does. But you agreed to the terms, Faith. It will work out. Trust me. Besides, he's hot, isn't he?"

Faith smiled.

"Yes, he's definitely hot. But that doesn't have anything to do with it," she said, though her body begged to differ.

It took an hour of soothing and cajoling, but Faith finally went home, feeling slightly better. She got the impression that Aaron hadn't liked her one bit. Well, she didn't need the likes of him to like her. If he didn't like her, she'd be well set. She'd have the money anyway. She'd deposited it. There was nothing he could do about that.

Cheering up, Faith did what she always did to cheer herself up: she went shopping. At least now her credit cards wouldn't complain. She had actual cash to spend!

It took a few more phone calls from Martha, but Aaron decided to go ahead with it. It was the logical decision. After all, the problems with Faith's behavior wouldn't be a problem for him.

Faith wouldn't be involved in his child's upbringing at all, if he so chose. On paper, she was perfect. Everything else... Well, he could deal with it, couldn't he? He would meet her once a week, of course. He would have to monitor the update, and he would be present at every single doctor's appointment. But after that, he wouldn't have to deal with Faith at all.

He could deal with appointments once a week for the term of a pregnancy. It wouldn't be that bad. At least she was a real pleasure to look at. She really was a beauty. A pity her personality didn't match with that, thought Aaron.

And so, the terms were arranged. Faith was a bit nonplussed by how impersonal it all seemed, but the point was that she was getting paid for all of it.

She woke up on The Day – insemination day – with butterflies in her stomach. Funny, thought Faith – she had been inseminated the regular way with no nerves, just fine. But artificial insemination made her all nervous and jittery.

Couldn't be any worse than her first time with Jimmy Davis, decided Faith, trying to cheer herself up.

She was going to have a child, if it took. If it didn't, she was going to try again. Faith had always imagined that the idea of trying for a child would be something that made her happy. The dreams had always included being in love with a man who loved her just as much, who wanted a baby just as much as she did.

It definitely hadn't included being impregnated with the knowledge that she was going to give up her child.

No, she wasn't even supposed to think of it as her child. That would be a slippery slope. Martha had warned her about it.

Martha would be there at the clinic. Faith hadn't really wanted her there. It felt odd. But Martha said that contractually, she was obliged to be there. It was all part of the service. Apparently, all Faith had to do was get on her back and let everybody else do all the work.

An hour later, it was done and Faith's face was burning. Aaron hadn't been there. Apparently, he was only going to see her at the first doctor's appointment. This part didn't need the father's attention. How odd things were. It had been sterile, scientific, completely devoid of all emotions – all in a day's work.

Now all Faith could do was hope that it had worked, because she didn't want to do that again. It had been mortifying. She wouldn't wish it on anybody.

She got out the list of things she was supposed to avoid and whistled. There sure were a lot of things. The rest of the vodka was obviously useless. She'd known that. But she hadn't realized that there were specific cheeses she wasn't supposed to have. Or fish. She couldn't have tuna? But she loved tuna melts!

Still, she thought, looking at the shoes and bags she'd bought, as well as the brand new tablet, it wasn't all bad. Not spending so much on food meant that she had lots to spend on all kinds of lovely new stuff! That was a good thing.

Besides, Aaron had set up an expense account for her at Whole Foods. She could order whatever she liked and it would be brought to her doorstep. Everything could be done online. This also meant that he could monitor what she was eating, which was a bit creepy, but she supposed she was like an investment for him to protect now. Fair enough, she figured.

Well, it would take about three weeks to know if it had worked. She might as well relax and get some reading done. She was a lady of leisure now.

Except it didn't take three weeks. In two weeks, Faith was doubled over her sink in the morning, puking her organic cereal and, apparently, trying her best to get rid of her damn intestines.

After about half an hour of hugging the toilet, she managed to drag herself to the bedroom and chug a glass of water. Big mistake – she lurched to the bathroom again to resume her affectionate camaraderie with the toilet.

After another half an hour, Faith was exhausted. Morning sickness wasn't supposed to start quite so early, was it? She either had a really bad case of food poisoning thanks to all the Whole Foods crap, or she was definitely knocked up and not going to have an easy pregnancy.

Nine months of this – Faith nearly fainted at the thought.

Maybe it was food poisoning. She'd read about bagged salads not being washed thoroughly and all that. Maybe that had been the problem. She wasn't even supposed to know if she was pregnant for a good while yet. She wasn't supposed to even get her period for another three days!

But Faith knew, in her heart, that she was definitely pregnant. She had already got five pregnancy test kits. She couldn't use any of them yet – it was far too early. Maybe she could go to the doctor and see if she could get something for this. Women had been bearing children for so long. Surely they didn't all go through this? There must be something she could have for it.

Desperate, she looked through the many pregnancy books she had bought. Apparently, salt crackers worked for some women. They felt like they weren't dying if they had some of that.

Faith didn't think she had any salt crackers. Did Whole Foods not have salt crackers? They must. She probably hadn't seen them. She needed to bulk order salt crackers.

Before she could finish the thought, she was back in the bathroom, hugging that damn toilet again.

She was going to die.

There was nothing else to be done about it. She called Martha.

"Crap," muttered Faith weakly. There was no answer.

Faith saw Aaron's card and hesitated. Should she? Maybe she should. It wasn't part of the contract, and she couldn't definitively say that she was pregnant, though she knew that she was. She had to be.

But she had nobody else to call. Nobody else knew what she was doing, that she was a surrogate. Faith was reluctant to call, but she thought nearly dying trumped embarrassment, and dialed.

"Hello?"

He sounded irritated. Faith barely had the energy to croak hello.

"It's me, Faith."

"Faith, is everything all right?"

"No, everything is most definitely not all right. I'm either pregnant or dying. Maybe both."

Concern and alarm were evident in Aaron's voice now.

"Faith, what's wrong?"

"I just spent an hour hugging the toilet, that's what's wrong."

"Are you saying you have morning sickness? Isn't it a bit early for it? Have you taken the test?"

"I've eaten nothing but healthy crap since that day. I have had absolutely nothing dodgy to get food poisoning. It's too early for the test. But I swear I'm definitely pregnant."

Aaron was quiet for a moment.

"Do you need me to send somebody to take you to the doctor?"

Aaron realized how callous that was as soon as he said it. It was his child that she was carrying, after all.

"No, I'll come there within half an hour and take you to the doctor. If you've been throwing up for that long, you might be dehydrated. We'll need to get you checked out. Wait there."

Before Faith could say anything, he'd hung up.

Fine, thought Faith. She'd wait there. Not as if she had anywhere to go.

She nearly crawled to the kitchen and poured herself about half a glass of juice.

Bad mistake. The smell of orange juice could, apparently, make her puke now.

Resigned, she just stayed in the bathroom until she heard a knock on her door. With great difficulty, she managed to drag herself to the door and open it. She looked a fright and she knew it. But she was past caring. She just wanted to stop feeling so sick.

Aaron took one look at her and slipped his arm around her, steadying her as he supported her to the car.

This was not looking good. She looked so fragile, nothing like the sassy woman he'd met earlier. Aaron was surprised at the tenderness he felt, but he reached for her hand and took it. He knew, without a doubt, that she was carrying his child.

It made all the difference in the world.

Chapter 5

A week later, Faith had all the proof she needed, apart from spending half her mornings on the cool bathroom floor. She had the little stick that said she was definitely pregnant. She considered calling Aaron to tell him that, but she wasn't sure if she should.

He had been very sweet that day when she'd called him to take her to the doctor. Of course, the doctor had basically told her to calm down and have fluids until Aaron had made his presence felt. Then, suddenly, she was treated with politeness and deference. He had held her hand, treated her tenderly, bought her all the groceries she needed, and dropped her back home.

She hadn't heard from him since then. Faith quite accepted that she had imagined the moment they'd had, when he'd held her hand. But she'd needed that reassurance then. She was grateful for it. During her worst moments of sickness, she found herself remembering that and being just a little comforted.

She picked herself up from the bathroom and kept the pregnancy test in a little box.

Faith was feeling a bit better, and decided to go for a short walk. It was cold, but bracing. She wondered if they'd have a white Christmas – that would be nice. But she spent Christmas with family, usually, and they didn't know that she had signed up to be a surrogate. How was she going to deal with that?

Sighing, Faith bundled up and decided to go and get herself a cup of really nice tea. She deserved a treat, though most treats were outlawed by the list of forbidden substances that Aaron had sent along. Faith resented his highhanded manner, but she did agree with the sentiment behind it. Her craving for sugar would need to take a backseat. The baby's best shot at health would require her to limit sugar drastically. The lack of caffeine was beginning to drive her mad, but she could handle it.

Faith went on to have a surprisingly fun day. She celebrated her pregnancy with more shoes, and then some more shoes because she figured she'd need bigger boots when her ankles were swollen in the winter. Though it was far too early for it, Faith knocked herself out shopping for some maternity clothes, too. They were so cute! A lot of the baby doll dresses would probably work later, too, when she was losing the baby weight.

Finally, when she swiped her card in the evening, Faith realized that she might have gotten a bit carried away. She now had barely enough to make rent next month. A moment of panic was firmly handled, and she carelessly hailed a cab to go home. She was carrying Aaron Matthews's child. The kid might as well get used to the luxury of hailing cabs and so on as early as possible.

For the next few days, Faith didn't do much more than read all the books she'd been stockpiling. She did, however, take a few breaks to order more maternity clothes and a whole set of new bras for when her boobs got bigger. It was, she justified to herself, a legitimate concern.

The last transaction, to her shock, was turned down because she'd wiped her account clean. Pouting, she canceled the order. She didn't have to worry. Rent was paid for the month and she didn't have to worry about food.

Besides, she'd be meeting Aaron in two days. She could get some more money from him quite easily. He could spare it.

The next morning, after her customary toilet-hugging routine, Faith went for her walk as usual. But this time, when she got back, she stared at the building's front door for a whole minute before she realized what she'd done.

"Shit!" muttered Faith.

She had locked herself out. She didn't have the key.

The spare key was with Martha. Her phone, however, was inside.

"It's all right, I just need to be buzzed in," she told herself and pressed a few buttons at random.

"Go away!"

"Look, I just need…"

"I don't give a fuck, fuck off!"

Well, that was neighborly. Maybe she could track down Jackass John and get the spare key from him. But she needed a phone for that. He didn't stay there.

Right, the building manager. The building was supposed to have one. She pressed the buzzer for the manager and got absolutely nothing.

So there she stood, getting colder and colder, feeling like a complete idiot.

Now what was she supposed to do?

She took deep breaths. She would need to find a locksmith. But she didn't have her phone and her neighbors were not neighborly, not in the least.

There was only one thing to do. She would have to break the lock. Faith knew how to do that. The door was flimsy. She just needed a crowbar. Determined, Faith walked out to a nearby construction site, borrowed one, and walked back to the building. Calmly, she jimmied the door open, walked back to the construction site, gave the crowbar back with a wide smile and went back home.

Once inside, walked up to her apartment and made herself breakfast.

Jackass John was going to have a fit when he saw the door, thought Faith with a grin. He couldn't prove she'd done it. The best part about New York was that nobody gave a rat's ass what anybody else was doing.

Still, she couldn't get rid of the slightly jittery feeling inside her. She would go out and spend the day at a bookshop, decided Faith. Not like she could buy anything, but it would still be fun.

Faith soon managed to forget about her troubles and have a wonderful time, but when she got home, she had a rude shock waiting for her – her things piled out in the hallway of her apartment, with an envelope on top.

Trembling with rage and helplessness, Faith opened it and read. It was an eviction notice, with immediate effect.

"No fucking way," muttered, and tried to open the door to the apartment.

The bastard had changed the lock! He couldn't just do that – he couldn't just kick her out like that. Property damage, what the fuck! She'd just broken open the door because she couldn't get in! She could pay for that.

Well, she couldn't right now, but she could pay for it soon enough.

Furious, she called Jackass John.

"Hello?"

"Mr. Nolan…"

"Ms. Richards. I tried to contact you all day, but you weren't reachable."

"You can't just throw me out like that! You have to give me time to find another place, at the very least. This isn't legal!"

"If you check your lease, Ms. Richards, you will see that I can do this, at my discretion, in case of property damage. You broke the front door."

"You have no proof that I did it!"

"I talked to the man you borrowed the crowbar from, Ms. Richards. I'm sorry, but you have to find some other place to live. If you don't get rid of the things cluttering up the hallway in twenty-four hours, I shall be left with no choice but to donate all of it to Salvation Army. If they'll take that crap."

"You can't do this!" screeched Faith.

"I might not have if I liked you, Ms. Richards, but I don't, and I can."

He hung up on her. The bastard hung up on her.

Faith stared at her stuff and her phone for a while, wondering what the hell she was supposed to do. Finally, she came to the conclusion that there was only one thing she really could do. She packed what she needed for a couple of days, and everything that could be stolen, into a duffel bag, standing out there.

Trying not to let the threatening tears overwhelm her, she walked out and hailed a cab. The cabbie raised his eyebrows when she gave him the address.

"Sure, lady," he said, shrugging when she glared at him.

Faith barely managed to pay him the fare. She was completely and utterly broke by then.

She let a little bit of resentment leak through when she saw the veritable mansion where Aaron Matthews lived. She had been kicked out of her crappy apartment, and look where the rich bastard lived.

The gate was open. That was, surely, a lapse in security.

Faith trudged up the driveway that seemed to never end, and finally got to the front door. She pressed the buzzer and kept it pressed down.

The door opened, and a very grumpy, but still handsome Aaron stood there.

"Faith? What're you doing here?"

"I need a place to stay."

Aaron didn't quite understand.

"What do you mean?"

"Look, I need a place to stay. It's freezing. Can you bloody let me in or do I have to do this standing out here?"

Silently, he stood aside. Faith swept in as if she had all the confidence in the world. But inside, she was quaking. Faith couldn't quite grasp what had happened. She was homeless.

"What happened?" asked Aaron, finally.

"I was kicked out by my landlord."

"Why?"

"Does it matter?" asked Faith, angry, but went on anyway. "I broke the lock of the building's front door. I was locked out in the morning. I tried buzzing, but nobody answered. The building manager wasn't there. My phone was inside. So I got a crowbar and broke the lock instead of freezing and risking bronchitis. I went out for the day. When I came back, all my stuff was in the hallway. The lock had been changed on the door, and there was an envelope there. I'd been evicted. I called the bastard and told him he couldn't do it, but he pointed out that he just had."

Faith took a deep, shuddering breath.

Aaron just stared at her. He could see that she was shaken, even if she was trying to hide it. He could understand and respect that – she didn't want to expose her vulnerability. He'd never been able to let weakness show, either.

"Why didn't you go to a hotel?"

Faith just gave him an incredulous look.

"You think I can afford to go to a hotel? If I had money to burn like that, do you think I'd be pregnant right now with your baby?"

"But you got your first check from me. It was quite generous!"

"I spent it."

Aaron gaped.

"You spent all of it?"

"I needed to get maternity stuff," said Faith defensively.

"You could've started a small maternity clothes shop with that!"

"Oh, shut up! What do you know about having to pinch pennies until it hurts to even catch a cab! I need a place to stay."

Aaron waged an intense battle with himself.

"Have you had dinner?" he asked, stalling.

"No."

"I'll get you something. Wait here."

He talked as if he was afraid she'd steal the silver if he let her wander around. Offended, Faith got up and walked around.

It was a nice place, really. It looked a bit too stiff and wasn't quite comfortable enough. It needed some clutter, something personal. But the pale green with wine red accents worked very well. It was elegant and smart. It just needed some humanity.

Funny, thought Faith. She could say the same about the owner of the place.

"In here," called Aaron.

Curious, she followed his voice and found herself walking through a formal dining room and into a kitchen that looked like something out of a 'perfect home' catalog. She wondered if anybody actually cooked there. But the smell of pasta was enough to nearly make her cry.

Ravenous, she sat down at the breakfast nook and ate greedily. Aaron watched her eat and wondered if she'd been eating properly.

Slowly, he came to the only real conclusion: he would have to let her stay with him. For one thing, he was no longer certain that she could take care of herself. If she stayed with him, he could be sure that she was taking care of herself and his baby.

Anyway, she would have to stay the night. It wasn't like he could kick her out.

"You can stay in the guest room for tonight," said Aaron.

Faith couldn't hide the sigh of relief. That little hint of vulnerability softened Aaron a bit too much.

He knew he was going to regret this.

"You can stay here until you get back on your feet, as long as you follow the house rules."

Faith knew she should be grateful, but the mention of house rules irritated her.

"Bed time at nine?"

She meant to be sarcastic, but to her surprise, Aaron grinned.

"Ten is good. Early nights should be good for the baby. Now, I need to get some work done. I assume you have more stuff? Of course you do. I'll send somebody to pick it up for now. But you should look into finding another place soon. I assume you want your space and your life."

"I can't afford a new place now. I'll have to beg to get my deposit back. I don't know if I'll even get it. The landlord is an asshole, anyway. He hit on me right when I was moving in and I wasn't receptive. He's had it in for me since then. I… Aaron, I'm broke. I can't afford to find another place until I get a job."

Faith was mortified. She was actually begging, but what choice did she have? Everything she'd said was the truth. She couldn't afford to find a new place.

Aaron sighed.

"We'll see how it goes. For now, settle in, and get some rest. You can start looking for a job soon. Or maybe you could consider moving in with your family. Surely you must have family? I read your medical history, and it says that your parents are still living, and have no hereditary ailments. You can stay here for now, but you should reach out to them, see if you can move in with them. I'm sure you want to be with your family during this time."

Faith made a noncommittal sound in reply. She still hadn't told her parents about this whole thing. If he thought she was going to turn up on their doorstep, he'd better think again.

Faith was so tired that she barely took in the opulence of the beautifully decorated bedroom with its attached bathroom. It was so big that the entire apartment she'd just been kicked out could easily have fit into it. She managed to change into a huge T-shirt and fell into bed. She was fast asleep in about two minutes.

*****

The next morning, Aaron woke up at six as usual, ready to hit the home gym. As he walked out of his room, though, he heard a sound that was very unusual in his home at that time.

It sounded as if somebody was dying.

Faith!

Aaron walked to her bedroom door and knocked on the door.

"Faith? Are you in there?"

There was no answer, but he heard the sound of really awful heaving, followed by a moan of pure desperation.

Gingerly, he pushed the door open and walked in. The bathroom door was open.

Faith was sitting on the bathroom floor, literally hugging the toilet, her face resting against the cool ceramic side of it. She looked deathly pale and her eyes were glassy. Her hair was bundled in a messy bun.

He hadn't known that her chocolate skin could look so waxy. He was about to dial 911 when Faith tried to smile.

"Hi," she croaked, but that's all she got out before she started heaving again.

There was only one thing he could think of doing. He got a towel and moistened it. Walking to the bathroom, he sat down next to Faith and held her hair back as she heaved again. Softly, he wiped her face with the towel.

"Thanks," whispered Faith, far too sick to be embarrassed.

"That doesn't look like fun," said Aaron.

"And the prize for the understatement of the day goes to..."

Aaron chuckled, despite himself. Finally, he was seeing some of that sense of humor that Martha had been talking about.

Abandoning his workout, Aaron stayed with her until Faith finally declared that she'd be fine. Aaron was dubious.

"Are you sure? Maybe we should go to the doctor."

Faith's belligerence came back as the sickness faded.

"It's just morning sickness. Just like a man, to get so panicked about it. I'm fine. Now would you mind leaving so that I can have some privacy?"

Aaron got up stiffly. What a prickly woman!

"I was trying to help."

"You want to help, you try being pregnant. Now, about that privacy?"

"You needed help."

"I've been managing just fine on my own, thank you very much."

"Yes, so well that you were kicked out by your landlord and you had nowhere to go!"

"That wasn't my fault. It's not my fault that Jackass John is such a jackass. And as for the help, any decent person would help somebody who's obviously in distress. What do you want for it, a cookie? You helped me deal with morning sickness. Well, I'm carrying your baby, so I'd say you're pretty much supposed to do that. So you can get off that high horse, rich boy."

Aaron couldn't believe just how ungrateful Faith was. With difficulty, he reined in his anger.

"I have to be at work by eight. If you need anything, you can call Mike. His phone number is on the refrigerator. It's also programmed into the house phone. Karen will be here by ten. She's the housekeeper. She makes meals and keeps them in the fridge. If you'll tell her what you feel like having, she'll make it for you. But the menu for the week has been decided, for dinner. Try to find a useful way of keeping yourself engaged. The liquor cabinet is locked."

Faith's mouth fell open at the last bit.

"You think you need to lock your liquor cabinet or I'll drink when I'm pregnant? You're an insufferable bastard, do you know that?"

"You seem to be very irresponsible, and I'm taking no risks. You are carrying my child, after all. Please consider my suggestion to get in touch with your family. I will see you later."

Faith held her tongue as he walked out.

What a way to start their living arrangement together, thought Faith. The man was insufferable and he thought she was a selfish, rude, irresponsible bitch. Well, thought Faith, they'd have to deal with each other for a while. She couldn't see another choice.

For a minute, Faith considered moving in with Martha, but she dismissed it immediately. She couldn't stand Martha's boyfriend. At least here, there was enough room to avoid each other.

Over the next few days, Faith and Aaron figured out a routine to keep out of each other's way – except in the mornings and late evenings.

Aaron soon figured out Faith's pattern. The pregnancy was giving her hypersensitivity to smells, so he switched all the household cleaning supplies to something neutral. He made sure that the kitchen was stocked with everything that could possibly help morning sickness. He noticed what she liked to read and ordered books for her. He gave her an Amazon gift card to download as many e-books as she wanted.

Aaron did everything he could to make the woman carrying his child comfortable. If Faith was stressed, it might stress the baby. He didn't want that. From his reading, he'd seen that the first trimester was often the most difficult and the most dangerous for the baby. He would do everything in his power to make sure Faith was comfortable. But he wanted her out of his home. Her vulnerability in the mornings made him feel drawn to her. Her prickliness at all other times infuriated him.

But Faith found Aaron confusing. He was giving her everything she needed, but he was also so aloof – he was obviously doing all of it despite his dislike for her. That annoyed her. He had decided that he disliked her despite not even taking the time to get to know her.

Well, the arrangement suited her. She had her space. As long as she could deal with the morning, she'd be fine. She knew that she was almost a month along now, and she was more than happy.

But that was soon about to change.

Chapter 6

Faith had been living with him for a week. Aaron was going to have a stern conversation with her that day. Dave had pointed out that this whole thing was going haywire, and he was right. He had chosen to have a child in this unconventional way because he didn't want to deal with arrogant, abrasive, gold-digging, vapid women.

He now had a woman who ticked all of those columns, living with him. It obviously could not go on. She needed to find a place to live. He wasn't running a hotel.

But when he walked in, the house was eerily quiet. His first reaction was annoyance. Where was Faith? If she'd gone out, she should've let him know.

He walked to her room and saw her stretched out on her bathroom floor.

He was swamped by fear, and it wasn't all for his baby. He didn't have room to consider that.

"Faith... Faith, come on, wake up."

Faith stirred and moaned. Aaron carried her carefully and laid her on the bed. As he wiped her face with a cool towel, he hit speed dial and called the doctor. Demanding tersely that the doctor come immediately, Aaron cut the call, without a doubt that he would be there.

Faith opened her eyes.

"Aaron…"

"I'm here. Don't worry, you'll be fine. You'll both be fine. The doctor's coming."

"The sickness wouldn't stop today. Then I got these cramps… They hurt so much. There was no bleeding, though. I think I just need to eat and drink something. Got dizzy. But baby's fine," whispered Faith.

"Shhh, don't worry about that now. You'll be fine."

His eyes were wild with worry as he ushered the doctor in to her. But the doctor, with his hearty, no-nonsense manner, reassured him immediately.

"No, it's fine. Don't worry about it. It's just your body preparing for your pregnancy. Kind of loosening up to make room, you know? You're young and fit, it happens quite often in the first trimester. You're not miscarrying or anything."

The relief that filled the room was palpable.

"Are you sure, Dr. Andrews?"

Faith smiled weakly. It was the first time she was seeing Aaron so completely uncertain of himself. It was endearing.

"Yes, of course. Tomorrow, come in for a scan, and we'll just make sure. But this is completely normal. Nothing to worry about."

After the doctor left, Aaron sat down next to Faith.

"I'll spend the night here. Just in case you need anything."

Faith smiled.

"You don't have to. You heard the doctor, I'm fine."

"Nevertheless," whispered Aaron and brushed her hair back from her forehead.

Settling down in a comfortable chair beside the bed, he watched her sleep. She looked small and sweet as she slept. No matter how prickly Faith had been when he met her, she was handling the pregnancy with far more grace than he'd expected. She was brave, and sweet, and obviously loved the child they were making. That, supposed Aaron, took courage when she knew that she would have to give it up.

Aaron made up his mind. He would go to work the next day after the ultrasound, and make all the arrangements he needed to. Faith needed him to be home. He couldn't leave her alone.

Faith knew nothing of his decision as they were driven to the clinic for her checkup. She thought he was being extremely unfeeling, spending the entire time on his tablet.

She tried to look at him without prejudice. He was handsome. She was attracted to him when he was being kind to her. But – and here was a problem she hadn't quite admitted to herself for about a month now – when she wasn't being sick like a dog, the pregnancy was making her horny. That made her want Aaron, since she couldn't exactly go and date somebody else when she was carrying Aaron's baby. She was also living under his roof, which made it even more difficult.

She probably should move out, admitted Faith though only to herself, but how could she, when she didn't have anywhere to move to?

To her surprise, he set the tablet down and took her hand as they got to the clinic. He held her hand as they waited their turn, too. He looked nearly as nervous as she felt. She squeezed his hand reassuringly.

By the time Faith was on the table, her still flat tummy exposed, Aaron looked so nervous he was nearly green. Faith had to bite back a grin. He looked like she had a couple of hours ago when she'd been hugging the toilet as usual.

The technician and the doctor made small talk, but Aaron wasn't very receptive. Feeling calm, Faith responded to all their questions and relaxed. Seeing Aaron so freaked out was relaxing her, oddly enough.

She felt his hand cover hers as they did the ultrasound.

"Everything seems fine. Nothing to worry about at all. Do you want to hear the heartbeat?"

Aaron's hand tightened on hers. They both nodded.

The moment the heartbeat filled the room, everything changed. Faith felt everything change. She was going to have a baby. She was giving life.

Tears in her eyes, she turned to Aaron and saw the awe on his face. He looked at her, and to her surprise, without a word, bent down and kissed her forehead.

As they left, Faith was a mess of emotions. She didn't want to think about what would happen when she gave up the baby. But she couldn't deny the attachment she felt at that moment — not just to the baby, but also to Aaron.

He hadn't let go of her hand.

When they were in the car, he finally spoke.

"I have to go to work now. I'll drop you at home before I do. I'm taking two weeks off after that, to make sure you're okay. The doctor said your morning sickness might get worse and you might need to stay in bed. You obviously cannot move out until we're sure you can take care of yourself. I can't leave you alone until then, either. So I'll be there."

Faith was astonished.

"But your work…"

"It'll go on. I can do most of it from home when I need to."

"I don't need you to babysit me."

"But I need to be there."

Faith said nothing to that. But now, along with being horny, she was filled with tenderness.

This wasn't supposed to happen. But maybe they could be friends. She just needed to keep the horny under control, and they could be friends with each other. That would be good, wouldn't it?

What could possibly go wrong?

*****

Three days later, Faith was more confused than ever. Aaron was being perfect – the perfect everything. He was still up before her and waiting for when she staggered to the bathroom. He brought her the food she liked. He had meals with her and he didn't snap at her.

Surprisingly, she didn't snap at him, either.

Then came the biggest surprise.

"I'm taking you out for dinner tonight."

Faith raised her eyebrows.

"Every smell in the world seems to make me sick. Do you really think a restaurant is a good idea?"

"Trust me. We both need to get out of the house. I'll handle it. Don't worry."

The quick grin made her heart beat just a bit faster. He had been the perfect gentleman to her, but she'd started wishing he wouldn't. The pregnancy-horny simply wouldn't go away, and now she was beginning to actually like the guy. She was already thinking of the evening as a date.

Faith spent a good hour getting ready. All the clothes she got – finally, some use out of them!

Faith wanted to knock Aaron's socks off. If it was a date, she definitely wanted to be kissed good night. If Aaron was the only man she could see for the next few months, she at least wanted to jump his bones. She was already pregnant with his child. What did she have to lose?

His reaction pleased her when she did come out.

"Faith, you look..."

With a smile, she walked to him and did a twirl.

"I almost have a baby bump. See?"

Taking his hand, she placed it on her stomach, sliding it gently up and down for him to feel how her belly was beginning to show.

She looked up at him with a smile and saw the look in his eyes before he could mask it.

SaucyRomanceBooks.com/RomanceBooks

It was desire – she recognized desire when she saw it in a man. In that moment, Faith didn't care about anything else. She needed to feel wanted. She needed to feel him.

His hand was still on her belly and his fingers were moving gently. She felt his touch all the way down to her toes. The warmth as her blood heated and hummed under his touch, left her with no choice at all.

"Aaron," she whispered, and leaned towards him.

Aaron saw her moving towards him, her lips parted so slightly, and he couldn't help himself. All the tenderness he'd been feeling turned into something far more potent. She was beautiful. She was carrying his child.

He wanted her.

Before good sense could prevail, he was pulling her closer, and he took her lips in a long, soft kiss that made Faith's head spin.

His lips were firm, but soft. She felt as if she'd been starving and had finally been given what she needed. Greedily, she parted her lips and traced the shape of his with her tongue, urging him to give her more.

She moaned in triumph and delight as he pulled her closer to him, his lips passionate and urgent now. She felt his hands move up her body to press her against him. His hands were on her back, roaming, moving down to cup her bottom and pull her even closer.

Faith moaned his name against his lips as he kissed her fervently. Hearing his name said in that breathy whisper made him kiss her again and again. Faith felt his lips move down her neck, finding that spot where her blood hammered, felt his tongue there.

His hands moved up her side to cup her breasts, so full and sensitive now, and she whimpered. His hands brushed against her nipples, again and again, and Faith whimpered his name over and over again.

"You're beautiful. You're so desirable," whispered Aaron as his lips found hers again, his tongue sliding along hers intimately as his hands pushed her breasts up, pulling the deep neck of her dress down.

He looked at that large, perfect, dark-tipped breast. Faith held her breath as he looked at her and felt her need grow wilder. She felt his mouth close on her nipple, felt his tongue lick her gently and she urged him on, her hand on the back of his head.

She didn't know where it would've ended, but his phone rang.

It barely penetrated the little bubble in which they were. But on the fourth ring, he seemed to snap back.

He stood up abruptly. Suddenly feeling cold and a bit bereft, Faith pulled her dress up as he took the call. With the blood roaring in her ears, she hardly heard what he said.

When he turned to her again, she had tears in her eyes.

"Faith," he whispered, his face gentle again.

"I... I'm sorry. I didn't mean..."

He pulled her into his arms.

"I know. I didn't mean to, either. Do you want us to pretend that never happened, and go out? Or would you like to stay in?"

Was he offering to stay in and make love to her, wondered Faith's wild mind. Probably not.

Anyway, she wanted to go out. She was getting cabin fever.

"I... Let's go out."

Did she see disappointment, before he masked it cleverly? But he nodded, and they were on their way.

It was the best evening Faith had ever had. He'd booked an entire restaurant so that there would be no smells she disliked. He had ordered the only thing she could eat without throwing up – a cheese omelet with a salad.

But all Faith could think about was what she had felt when he'd held her and touched her. Sure, some of it was just the pregnancy hormones. She had needs, and none of them had been met for far too long. Aaron had definitely not been on any dates since she'd moved in, either. But she'd felt something more than that.

Faith pushed that thought aside. Her life already had enough complications.

"It must be nice to be rich enough to do something like this," said Faith, and her voice was wistful, not derisive as usual when she referred to his money.

Aaron must've let his guard drop, because he told her the truth.

"I grew up poor. I know what it's like. So I never take my money for granted. I try to do what I can for the community, but the system doesn't let you help very much."

"You didn't inherit your money?"

Aaron laughed.

"God, no. Do you know how long it took for these old money bastards to even let me make deals with them? I had to play their game for far too long. Now I can buy and sell most of them multiple times, so I've got the last laugh."

Faith found herself warming to him, seeing herself on his side, against the world.

"Good for you. I never had the drive to make something of myself like you did, I suppose. I just wanted a paycheck so that I could buy all the books I wanted. I've always wanted to write a book, but then the publishing industry went to hell. I got one job at a publishing firm and they fired me. That was one time I definitely didn't deserve it – I just gave the boss's nephew's book, which I didn't even know was his nephew's book, an honest and very bad review. But the bastards blacklisted me after that. Couldn't get another job in the industry. So I took dead-end jobs to pay bills, and got sick of it. It's not a very good story," confessed Faith.

But Aaron felt like he finally understood why this beautiful woman with her good heart and her strength was as prickly as she was. She'd had her dream crushed, and she'd given up.

For the rest of the meal, they didn't talk about anything that personal. But Aaron told her funny stories about his childhood that made her laugh, and like him even more.

By the time they were on their way home again, Faith felt like she'd been on a wonderful date. Being chauffeured home was a nice touch. She took his hand and smiled at him. When he leaned towards her and kissed her, it felt like the most natural thing in the world. She felt herself melt into him as those wonderful hands stroked her body, those lips moved over hers, so gently and tenderly that she felt as if she were floating on a cloud.

"Aaron," she whispered as she felt his hands move over her back, pressing her close to him as he kissed her, his tongue tracing the shape of her lips. She parted her lips, welcoming him, and she gave him her tongue. She felt him suck on her tongue gently. She felt that tug all the way down her body. She felt it as a liquid pull deep in her belly, and wrapped her arms around him.

When they got home, she found herself straddling him, grinding on him, his hands in her hair. She was kissing him as if she could never get enough. They barely realized when the car came to a stop for a good two minutes.

They broke apart, breathless.

"I want you," whispered Faith.

She felt his hands cup her breasts and squeeze gently.

"Inside. Bedroom," said Aaron.

They made it inside, and didn't care if anybody saw them. They stumbled, their hands full of each other, to the door.

Aaron pressed Faith against the door, kissing her madly as his hands roved over her.

Faith pressed herself against him and felt the evidence of his desire for her. She thrilled as she felt him, hard and long, pressed against her.

"Inside," groaned Aaron again, fumbling open the door.

He picked her up, kicked the door shut, and walked to the bedroom. Faith wrapped her arms around his neck and kissed his cheek, moving to his ear and slipping her tongue inside, making him groan.

He laid her down on the giant bed and moved over her. Faith's urgent hands were pulling off his jacket and his tie, fumbling with his buttons.

"How do I get this damn thing off?" muttered Aaron, making Faith laugh breathily. Slithering under him, she undid the hook and wiggled out of her dress.

She lay there, in her black lacy bra and panties, looking so beautiful that Aaron felt his mouth go dry.

Quickly, Aaron got rid of the rest of his clothes and moved next to her. He wanted to make her feel more. He wanted to watch her rise to the peak and tumble for him.

As he watched, she undid the front clasp of her bra and flicked it open. For the second time, he saw her breasts, but this time, he knew he didn't have to stop. He reached out, his fingers finding both her nipples and rubbing gently. He pulled on them slightly and watched as Faith's eyes closed, her head thrown back, her lips parted as she felt those little currents swamping her senses. He leaned down to kiss her, long, deep and passionate, as his hands cupped her breasts and squeezed gently.

Faith felt her breasts grow heavy and fill his hands. Her nipples were hard and taut, reaching for more. When he touched them, rubbed them, she moaned and sought his tongue. She wanted so much more. She wanted to feel his hard manhood deep inside her.

He broke that kiss and Faith moaned in protest. But then his mouth was on her breast, licking it softly, teasing her with little circles around her nipple, as his hand moved down over her ever-so-gently rounded body. Faith's legs fell apart, and his fingers moved down between her legs, tracing so lightly over her mound that she could barely feel it – but oh, how she felt it!

She was so wet, so hot, so needy for him that her hips moved and writhed, trying to make him touch her more. When he finally slipped her panties aside and touched her, moving along her lips so gently, so softly, Faith cried out her pleasure.

When his finger slipped deep inside her, moved deep inside her wet, velvet heat, Faith trembled. With his mouth on her breast, his finger finding that little nub of swollen flesh in her center that needed his touch, Faith felt herself climbing to the climax she needed.

His hands were relentless, those long fingers slipping deep in and out of her, until she was crying out for him. His mouth was merciless as he moved to her other breast and sucked on her nipple.

"Please," begged Faith as she felt the heel of his palm rubbing against her clit as his fingers moved faster, in and out of her, until she felt her body clench, coil, and shatter with pleasure so intense she felt like she couldn't hold it inside her.

Before she could recover, she felt him slide her panties down and move over her. She felt his heart beating against her, thundering his need. His lips were moving over her neck, down her torso, making her feel so much more that she thought she couldn't hold it all. She felt him kiss her belly tenderly and it made her breath catch, with more than pleasure.

Slowly, he made his way down her body, down her legs, finding little spots of pure pleasure that dazzled her even more. When he moved up her inner thighs, kissing and licking that sensitive, delicate, skin, her legs trembled.

"Aaron... Aaron, I can't!" gasped Faith as she realized where that skilled, perfect mouth was headed.

"Yes, you can. You will," said Aaron, and Faith felt his breath between her legs.

When his lips closed over her, licking her, kissing her, sucking gently, Faith's back arched off the bed. Her hands fisted in the sheets as she tried to hold on, but she couldn't. There was too much.

Closing her eyes, she let herself be driven up and over, taken over by him, by his skillful tongue that was intent on giving her pleasure.

Swiftly, he moved over her. Her body was still trembling when he braced himself over her, poised with his steel length at the entrance of her welcoming warm pussy.

"Look at me when I take you," whispered Aaron.

She kept her eyes on his as she felt his erection, long and thick and hard, poised against her wet, hot, needy entrance. She felt him push inside her, filling her, stretching her, and she gasped.

"Oh yes, don't stop," she whimpered as he sheathed himself deep inside her before pulling almost all the way out and thrusting back inside her.

"Oh God yes," whispered Faith mindlessly as his long, steel length pulsed and throbbed inside her. She wrapped her legs around him and her hips moved with him, urging him on.

"You feel so good, Faith. You're so hot and tight, so wet," whispered Aaron as he pushed as deep inside her as he could.

He wanted to go slow, and gentle, but he couldn't hold back. He thrust harder, and faster, until Faith was chanting his name, over and over again, as if she couldn't stop herself.

She felt herself climb up, reach for that peak of pleasure yet again, and she pulled him closer to her, covering his lips with hers, kissing him long and deep.

He gasped her name as he felt her body tremble and shudder as she found her climax again, holding still until he felt her tremors subside.

Then, desperately, he plunged deep inside her and emptied himself in her, his face buried against her neck.

Chapter 7

Faith woke up with that familiar gut-wrenching feeling that made her run to the bathroom. She registered, fairly vaguely, that she wasn't where she was used to waking up. By the time Faith remembered everything that had happened, she had resumed her affectionate companionship with the toilet, but a different one.

Even as she tried her best to get rid of her intestines, she noticed the master bathroom was beyond opulent. She needed to have a bubble bath there at some point.

Odd how she'd pretty much got used to the routine, thought Faith, and waited for Aaron to come and pat her on the back. It was only as she thought of that that she realized she was naked.

To her surprise, she felt shy.

After everything Aaron and she had shared the night before, there should be no room for shyness between them, at all.

But Aaron didn't come. Slowly, that feeling of aloneness swept over her. She was alone in the house.

In a few minutes, she was lying down on the cool tiles and wondering what was going on. She wasn't foolish enough to think that they were going to live happily ever after. When two adults in an unusually intimate situation live together for a while, things happened. It would've been a bigger surprise if nothing had happened, to be honest.

She could deal with that.

But Aaron's absence now hit her hard. She had come to depend on him. It was jarring to realize that. Faith was used to not depending on anybody. She made a fine mess of things quite often, but she didn't depend on anybody. She did it on her own, just like she picked herself up and went on by herself.

The idea that she'd gotten used to somebody else holding her hand while she did that didn't sit well with her, not at all.

This was a temporary arrangement. As soon as the baby was born, Aaron would be out of her life. She would have to go on as usual after that. She'd have more money than she'd ever had before, but at the moment, it wasn't money she wanted. It was the comfort of having Aaron beside her, telling her it was going to be okay, and that scared her.

That needed to change, decided Faith as she got herself up and walked to the kitchen to get some juice. For some strange reason, she could keep pomegranate juice down. She'd stopped wondering about odd things like that. It was apparently just part of the great mystery that was pregnancy.

As she sipped the juice, Faith took stock.

That morning was the first time Aaron hadn't been there in the last few weeks. It had happened right after they slept together. She wasn't a complete idiot, so she didn't think those two things were unconnected.

Either the man thought he'd crossed a line or he was scared that she'd expect too much of him. Whichever it was, Faith found herself mortified, and a bit angry.

If he thought that he'd crossed a line, he should've stayed there and talked to her about it. He could just arbitrarily draw lines and decide if he'd crossed them. There were two people involved in the situation, and she deserved to have her say.

Now, if he thought she'd expect too much from him, he was sorely mistaken. Faith had never tried to hold on to a man who didn't want her. She had her flaws and plenty of them. She was well aware of that. But she never tried to tie anybody down.

Even if she'd been so inclined, the man had a damn contract, didn't he? Even with the money he was going to pay her, it wasn't like she could ever afford to sue him! So what the hell was he afraid of? A man didn't get to be as successful as he was without dealing with conflict and getting through confrontations. He couldn't have run squawking like a chicken just because he thought they might have a fight!

"Dickhead," muttered Faith as she ate dry cereal – another thing she could keep down, miraculously, in the morning – and wandered off to find a book to read.

If he thought she was going to be clingy and demand attention just because they'd slept together, he was sadly mistaken. She could be as blasé as the best of them. When he came home, she would be so breezy that he would find himself wondering if the night before had actually happened.

Still, Faith couldn't help it – her heart did get a little bit heavier as the day went on. She kept her phone close by. Just in case, she told herself, she had an emergency and she needed to call for help. It was the sensible thing to do. But she knew, in her heart, that she kept it with her because she hoped that Aaron would call.

As the day went by and he neither called nor texted, Faith felt like her heart was weighed down with stones.

*****

"Come on, man, what the hell is wrong with you! I haven't seen you in weeks. You've been babysitting that damn surrogate of yours. Now you can't even seem to keep your mind on the contracts here!"

Dave had good reason to complain. Aaron had found himself strangely unable to concentrate.

He had snuck out of his own bedroom like a coward that morning. He had done so because he was a damn coward, and he was mortified to admit it.

What had he been thinking? Why the hell had he done something so completely stupid? He had slept with Faith.

No, sleeping was what they hadn't done much of until the crack of dawn. He had fucked her brains out.

The crudeness of that made him wince. He had made love to her, more tenderly than he'd ever done with anybody ever before, he admitted to himself.

What had possessed him to do such a thing? Now everything was complicated. Aaron avoided complications in his personal life.

One of the biggest reasons why he'd chosen the surrogate service was precisely because it wasn't complicated. You get matched with the right person, the insemination process is done under clinical supervision, you pay the fees and the extras, and that was supposed to be it.

Nothing about his current situation was simple. Everything to do with Faith was complicated.

He could hardly believe he'd let himself get into such a situation. He knew Faith had very little respect for what he did for a living, thought he wanted to think that last evening, they'd found a different kind of understanding.

He had finally begun to understand why Faith was such a bundle of contradictions. She was a dreamer – a dreamer and an optimist who'd been forced into situations that had jaded her. Now, with that new insight, he couldn't help but see how much her current situation could damage her in the long run.

Aaron had no doubts that Faith was strong. But her heart was fragile. Giving up this child would be a blow for her; a bigger blow, perhaps, than even she realized at the moment. And yet, he knew, without a doubt, that she had never even considered not facing that pain, because that was an essential part of her surprising integrity.

The woman drove him mad.

But the biggest reason why he'd snuck out of his home like a thief that morning was that he'd seen her sleeping there, looking like a dark and vengeful goddess, he'd been filled with tenderness. He'd wanted to hold her.

That was a weakness that could not be allowed. He couldn't deal with that. She was his surrogate. He couldn't develop feelings for her. What was he supposed to do, date the mother of his child but keep the child away from the mother?

What a fucking impossible situation!

"Aaron? Hey, man, come on!"

Aaron brought himself back to the present.

"Ah, sorry, Dave. I'm really not into it today."

"Color me shocked. What the hell is going on with you?"

He sighed and considered telling Dave just what was going on. After all, Dave was his oldest friend. If he couldn't confide in him when he was dealing with something like this, when could he?

"I did something incredibly stupid," admitted Aaron.

Dave waited, looking skeptical. Aaron wasn't known for doing stupid things. That was more Dave's thing.

"I slept with Faith."

"Faith... You mean the surrogate. You slept with your surrogate? The woman who's supposed to be having your child, for money?"

Dave looked like he was having trouble believing the words.

Irritated, Aaron shrugged.

"How many Faiths do I know? Of course that's what I meant. It's what I said."

"I… Wow, that is a horrible mistake."

Aaron was slightly taken aback. He knew that, but Dave and he often differed in their opinion of what constituted a horrible mistake.

"Seriously, Aaron. The woman is having a child for money. What do you think she's going to do now that she's sleeping with you? She's going to think that she's got it made, for the rest of her life!"

The idea was distasteful to Aaron.

"She's not like that," he snapped.

"Oh, really? Then why the hell is she renting her womb out for money? Come on, man, you can't think she's got some great ethical standard or anything. She got pregnant for money. Now she's sleeping with a billionaire. What do you think she's thinking?"

Put that way, it did seem extremely unsavory.

"It's not like that, Dave."

"Then what is it like? True love? Are we supposed to have a Disney theme song?"

Aaron's face tightened.

"Don't be ridiculous," he said sharply.

"Aaron, buddy, listen to me. You know I only have your best interests at heart, right? Always. So take my suggestion. Pay the woman off, get her another apartment, pay the rent yourself, and set her up there till she pops the kid out. Then take the kid, pay her what you owe her and a generous enough tip to keep her happy, and cut her out of your life. Keep everything professional. You can't help what's happened already, but don't do it again. I know her type, Aaron. She's a leech. She's just looking for an easy way through life. If she hadn't found a better paying pregnancy gig, she'd be a welfare queen. Don't get sucked in," warned Dave.

Aaron felt the bile rise as Dave said those ugly things. But he refused to consider why he wanted to break Dave's face for talking about Faith that way.

"I can take care of myself. I don't need you to stand in judgment over Faith. You don't know her, and you never will," he said, his tone cutting.

"I know that, and I mean no disrespect," assured Dave soothingly. "But right now, you're looking at her as the mother of your child, Aaron. When she's not carrying your baby, do you really think you will look at her and feel this way? Right now, you love your kid, obviously. Those feelings are being transferred to the woman who's carrying your child. Once you have your baby, do you really think you're going to feel so… protective about her?"

Aaron was silent. He wasn't sure he could answer that honestly.

"Besides," went on Dave relentlessly, "think of how you would've seen her if you'd met her somewhere. You would never have given her a second look!"

Aaron's lips twitched. That wasn't true. Faith was gloriously beautiful. Any man would give her more than a second look.

"All right," amended Dave, noticing the look, "you might have looked. But you wouldn't have been really interested in her.

You would've dismissed her as a lazy, entitled, whiny woman. You would've been right. Why do you think she's different now, other than the fact that she's carrying your baby? I'm telling you, get her out of your home."

Aaron kept his face carefully controlled.

"We have work to do, Dave. I have a lot of catching up to do. Maybe we can get back to it?"

Dave knew that tone. It meant that the topic was tabled, and it would only be reopened if and when Aaron felt it should be. He backed off immediately, but he hoped that Aaron had listened to him.

He only had his friend's best interests at heart. And he knew, with absolute certainty, that Faith was bad news. She couldn't be a part of Aaron's life. She would make him miserable. He would do whatever it took to make sure that she left his friend alone.

As the day went on, Aaron had to stop himself from calling Faith multiple times. She was all right, he assured himself. If she needed anything, she would have plenty of help. The hospital was required to notify him if Faith was admitted for anything, or even if she went in for a check-up without him. If she needed anything, she would call him.

But he needed something – he needed to hear her voice making an irreverent quip that made the world rest far more lightly on his shoulders. He wanted to see her smile. He wanted to feel the gently rounded belly under his hands and wonder at the life that grew there. He wanted to see her curled up on the window seat, reading a book, her hand resting protectively on her belly. He wanted to see the incongruity of Faith reading a grisly murder mystery with that gentle, serene smile on her face.

He just wanted to see her.

Warning bells were ringing in his head, so loud that he couldn't focus on anything else. What on earth was wrong with him? He was daydreaming about that damn woman instead of getting his work done, thought Aaron, closing his laptop in disgust.

Dave was right. This situation was well out of control. He had made a huge mistake, and he was sure that Faith would now have unreasonable expectations. He had absolutely no intention of being in her life in any way at all after the baby was born.

Then why, he wondered, did that determination make him feel so bereft, as if he was cutting joy out of his life?

Restless, he got up and paced the office.

He needed distance. He could not have a relationship with Faith. It simply wouldn't work. He couldn't have her living with him under such strained circumstances.

There was really only one thing to be done. He needed to get Faith out of there, even if it meant getting her a new apartment and hiring a companion.

*****

As the day went on, Faith got more and more restless. The situation was getting to her.

Even worse, she missed Aaron. She wasn't supposed to miss him. He was... Well, he was her employer, she supposed. He wasn't her boyfriend. He wasn't her husband. He might be the father of her unborn child, but that didn't mean anything, not in her situation.

It was just impossible.

Faith made up her mind. She needed to move out.

Except, thought Faith, deflated, that she didn't have anywhere to go. She still hadn't told her family about her situation. She didn't have any friends she could stay with. There was only Martha, and she hadn't told Martha about the new arrangement.

Come to think of it, Martha hadn't called her, either. That wasn't very nice of her. The least she could do was check up on her.

Impulsively, she called Martha.

"Faith, what's wrong? The last update I got was that everything was fine."

"Update? What update?"

"Why, Aaron has been sending me steady updates. He said that you'd moved in with him because your pregnancy has been rather difficult. I wanted to get in touch with you, but he was very insistent that I wait until you were ready to talk to me about it. It's very sweet, really, how he's become so protective of you. It's unconventional, but it seems to be working for you."

Faith finally managed to pick her jaw up from off the floor.

"Aaron has been giving you updates?"

"Well, yes. It's part of the contract that I be in touch with the surrogate, but he drafted his own contract, which gives him a lot more wiggle room. So, how are you?"

"I need a place to stay. I need to bunk on your couch or something."

There was silence from the other end.

"Faith, what's wrong?"

"I… Nothing's wrong. You know how this man is. He's being horribly overbearing and I can't stand it. I just need some space, Martha. Can I bunk with you for a few days? I should get my next check soon. I can get a new place then and move out. But for now, I need a place to stay."

"Faith! You mean you're with Aaron because you're homeless? What happened to your first payment?"

"I had bills," said Faith, defensively.

"Good God, Faith! Look, I'll get in touch with him and get him to pay you an advance soon. Until then, you can come and stay with me, of course. I'm alone for a week, anyway. You can sleep in the bedroom. I'll take the couch."

"You don't have to do that," said Faith, feeling conflicted.

"You're a pregnant woman, I can't make you sleep on the couch. When will you come?"

"Ah… I'll be there as soon as I can. I need to get my stuff together, get a cab… Just stuff. I'll be there by evening. Will you be home?"

"I'll be home from six. You don't have to rush or anything. You are taking care of yourself, right?"

"You know who I've been living with, right?" shot back Faith.

Martha chuckled.

"Right, of course. Well, then, I'll see you soon," said Martha, and they both hung up.

Faith was strangely reluctant to get a move on. She should pack, she told herself, and finally got to work doing just that.

She didn't pack most of her stuff. She just got her essentials together, throwing it all in a duffel bag. She got her prenatal vitamins and supplements, put them in another, smaller bag.

Now... She needed cab fare, realized Faith.

It was humiliating to know that she had to get the housekeeping petty cash for that. Feeling lowered, she scribbled a note asking Aaron to deduct that from her next check.

She considered just leaving, but that didn't seem right. Aaron was a good man, at the core of it all. He would absolutely freak out if he came home and didn't find her.

A note, decided Faith. She would leave a note.

Now she needed to write a note. What the hell was she even supposed to say?

Finally, she decided on a straightforward, no-frills little message.

Dear Aaron.

Thank you for your hospitality for the last few weeks. Believe me, I appreciate it. But I feel that it isn't right to impose on you this way. I believe I'm not capable of getting back on my feet, and I think it's time that I moved out.

You don't have to worry that I won't take care of myself. I will.

Anyway, I'm going to be with Martha for a few days, until I can find my own place. Well, you know that I can't afford to find my own place until you give me my next check, so I hope you'll give me an advance.

Again, thank you for everything. I wish you the best.

I will see you once a week, as promised, and look forward to it.

Yours,

Faith

She read it a couple of times, made a few minor adjustments, and nodded her head in satisfaction.

Good, that should work, decided Faith. It made no reference to their night together. He couldn't accuse her of overreacting. Besides, every word in that was true, so he couldn't accuse her of lying, either.

Perhaps she was lying by omission, but at least she hadn't snuck out of house and run away instead of facing him, like he had done!

Faith called a cab and told herself not to be silly when she felt a deep reluctance to leave the house. It wasn't home. It was definitely not her home. She would have a home again, soon.

For now, she was going to stay with her friend, and she would preserve at least some modicum of dignity and independence.

*****

When Aaron came home that evening, he had a speech all prepared. He was going to be frank and rational, and he would expect Faith to be reasonable.

He was fairly sure that it would take some fast talking to get her to be reasonable, but he knew he would prevail. He always did.

But when he opened the door, the moment he stepped in, he knew that the house was empty. His first reaction was blind panic. He was on the point of calling 911 when he saw the note propped on the coffee table.

He read it and felt unexplainable rage coursing through his body. Crumpling the piece of paper, he threw it violently away.

Faith was gone. That's what he'd wanted.

So why did he feel so empty inside?

Chapter 8

Faith was nervous. She told herself that she was being silly. It wasn't the first time she'd had to face a man she'd slept with. There was no reason to be nervous.

Martha fluttered around her like a nervous mother hen.

"Faith, are you sure you don't want me to come with you?" fretted Martha.

Faith shook her head. The idea of having an audience when she saw Aaron again made her feel sick.

Oddly enough, the morning sickness seemed to be dissipating a bit. It hadn't been that bad over the last week. But as if to make up for that, Faith felt more and more listless each day. She could hardly drum up any interest in anything.

She'd tried to start writing, but it hadn't worked.

Martha was beginning to come to the conclusion that she had made a huge mistake by asking Faith to be a surrogate. Her pregnancy was difficult enough. But her relationship with Aaron, if she could even use the word 'relationship' for that godawful mess, was putting an unbelievable strain on her.

The light seemed to have gone out of her eyes. Faith had always had such beautiful eyes that always shone. They glittered with anger or they sparkled with laughter, but they were never so empty.

Faith had been taking care of herself very well. Martha hadn't had to nag her to eat even the things she didn't like, but were good for her. But Martha knew that Faith had done all of that for the baby, not for herself.

Martha was beginning to dread the day Faith finally gave birth to that child. What would happen to her friend after that? She was so used to seeing Faith full of fire. This new fragility scared her.

It was all that damn bastard's fault, thought Martha as Faith considered makeup and decided it wasn't worth it.

Maybe she should wear makeup. She had bags under her eyes. But Faith couldn't see a reason to put that effort into her appearance. Aaron already knew what she looked like, at her best and her worst. At her worst, he had held her hand and given her comfort. At her best… Well, he had ravished her, and she had loved every single, solitary second of it.

But since then, he had barely talked to her. He had texted and emailed her every single day asking her how she was, but so impersonally – as if the only reason he was interested in knowing how she was doing was to figure out if the baby was fine.

She had made a huge mistake, thought Faith. Why had she even thought that he had any kind of real interest in her? Even worse was the realization that she missed him so much. She missed how he gently nagged her to eat well, or gave her the supplements she needed, or brought home whatever cravings she'd been dealing with.

It wasn't just because he had been so concerned and genuinely caring. There had been something more – there had been something precious in the way he had listened to her. She'd told him so much about herself. Faith had thought they'd reached a level of intimacy and understanding that had meant a lot to her.

But he had left that morning before she could wake up. He hadn't called her all day. Faith knew his moods and his reactions. Aaron had made his desire perfectly clear by what he hadn't done: he had wanted her gone because he felt what they did was a mistake.

Faith agreed, now.

For the first couple of days, Faith had lived in hope that he would come and take her home. Every time the doorbell rang, her heart had raced in hope that it was Aaron.

She'd weaved so many fantasy scenarios – ones where he was upset that she'd left, ones where he was angry but she forgave him because the anger came from a place of… love.

Even thinking the word made her feel as if her heart was being squeezed in a vice.

She had been falling in love with him.

She'd been lucky to get out when she did. If she'd stayed with him, she would've fallen far too deep before she realized what a mistake she was making. It would've been terrible.

As it was, she'd just managed to pull herself back from the brink, Faith assured herself, but she didn't really believe it.

"Stop stalling," Faith ordered herself.

Making her way to the street, she hailed a cab and gave him the address. She'd had to borrow money from Martha for that.

But surely Aaron would give her an advance! She'd emailed him and asked him for one. He hadn't really told her if he would – he had just given her the address where she should be for their weekly meeting, and said that he'd 'take care of it' then.

How many ways could he take care of it? She needed money. It wouldn't be a handout. It would be an advance.

She felt everything inside her tense as she reached and got out of the cab.

Faith didn't check the time. She knew that she was on time.

What a drastic change from the first time she'd met him!

Aaron was inside, waiting for Faith. He had a few things to say to her. First of all, there was a matter of respect. It was disrespectful to leave the way she did. He had a list of all the things she'd done wrong.

But when he saw her, everything he had planned to say just vanished from his mind.

She didn't look well, realized Aaron, with shock. She didn't have that jaunty swing of the hips, that slight bounce as she walked that announced she was ready to take on the world.

Faith didn't look like herself, and he felt like he'd been stabbed in the heart. It was all his fault. She had left, but he had left first. If he had stayed and talked to her in the morning, held her as he did every morning, all of this could've been avoided.

She seemed listless as she sat down in the chair facing him. When she smiled, there was no joy.

Aaron felt the guilt stab him again.

"Faith... You don't look well."

He could've bit his tongue to stop the words, but they wouldn't be stopped.

Faith chuckled mirthlessly.

"Why, thank you. I can't quite return the compliment."

Her heart was beating so hard that it was painful. It felt like a physical ache to see him sitting there, looking so perfect, so detached. How could she deal with this?

"Are you all right?" persisted Aaron.

Faith shrugged.

"You've been getting your daily health update. The next doctor's appointment is next week. I assume you will be there. I'm sure he'll give me a clean bill of health."

"That's not what I'm talking about."

"Isn't it?"

He sat back, pleased that he saw some of her old fire flashing in her eyes. He welcomed the anger rather than the emptiness he had seen earlier.

"I don't think I can tell you what you want to hear, Faith."

Faith glared at him.

"And what the hell do you think I want to hear?"

"I can't give you an advance."

Her mouth fell opened. She opened and closed it a couple of times, swallowed and tried again.

"Why not?"

"Because it seems clear to me that you haven't been taking care of yourself. I require you to take care of yourself, of course. So I cannot give you an advance, as I cannot trust you to do what's best for yourself. And the baby."

If looks could kill, Aaron would've been dead.

"What the bloody hell do you mean by that?"

Aaron let the mask slip for just a second and Faith saw the smoldering rage behind the seemingly relaxed man.

"I mean that you look like hell, Faith. You look like you haven't had a good night's sleep. You're pale and listless. I had to practically goad you into arguing with me!"

"So now you have a problem with me being civil?"

Frustrated, Aaron raked his fingers through his hair.

"You couldn't be civil if you were knocked unconscious," he muttered.

"And what the fuck do you mean by that? I've been sticking to all your terms, haven't I?"

People were beginning to stare.

"Be that as it may, it would be far more sensible to have this discussion where we won't attract so much attention. I don't know about you, Faith, but I'm not keen on having this whole thing in the tabloids tomorrow morning. Or on a damn gossip website now!"

"Where do you have in mind?" Faith spat the words out through gritted teeth.

Grabbing her elbow, Aaron pulled her to her feet and guided her outside, where, of course, a chauffeured limo was waiting for him.

"You won't have any of your billions left if you keep running up parking tickets like that," said Faith snidely.

She was seething. What a highhanded boor he was! She had changed her mind. She had had an incredibly lucky escape. Why on earth would she want this bastard in her life?

Aaron didn't dignify that with a response. Annoyed and irritated, she got in the car with him. What the hell was his game now?

"Aaron, what the hell do you want?"

Suddenly, her voice sounded weary. She didn't want to play games with him. She couldn't match his rules. She was out of her league.

All Faith wanted was to be left alone to live her life.

No, that wasn't true. What Faith really wanted was to jump the bastard's bones, fuck him silly, and leave him dazed. That way, he would be the one at a loss, not Faith.

To her surprise, he turned to her with gentleness and took her hand.

"Faith, you really don't look well. Oh, I know you're taking care of your health. You would never do anything to endanger the baby. But you don't look like yourself. You seem so... listless. The only time you had any life was when I was antagonizing you. I... You must know that I care for you, not just for the well-being of the baby. I want you to be well, Faith. I don't want to see you like this."

The kind consideration did what no harsh words could. Faith, to her mortification, found that tears were flowing down her cheeks.

"Shh, come now. It will all be fine. I promise. I know I handled it badly. But come with me now. I'll take care of you."

Faith was so exhausted that she barely registered how Aaron had apologized. That was not something he did every day. She knew that.

She was so tired and weary that even being taken care of sounded appealing. It would be nice to just let go and not worry about anything. She could… What was she thinking?

"What are you trying to say, Aaron?"

"Come home with me. I miss you, Faith."

The simple admission did more than any threat or bribe could. It made her heart quiver and let go.

He missed her. If that was all she could get, she would take that, because she had missed him so much that she felt as if her heart would just break.

"I missed you, too," she whispered, finally, as she felt the car slowing to a halt.

Aaron felt like he could finally breathe. He hadn't known how tense he'd been.

"Faith… If you don't want to come home with me, you don't have to. I… I was going to lease an apartment for you and give you that advance. I was going to let you go. That day, when I came back home, I was planning to tell you that. But you weren't home, and it wasn't just the house that felt empty. I felt empty, too."

Faith raised her eyes to his, only half believing what he was saying.

"You can still have that if that's what you want. If that's what will make you happy."

Was it? Was that what would make her happy?

No, realized Faith – Aaron made her happy. Being with him made her happy.

Feeling unaccountably shy, she leaned towards him to kiss him, so softly, so sweetly that Aaron felt like his heart was melting. He held her like she was the most precious thing in the world.

"I'm coming home," said Faith, and those simple words gave him the world. It gave him a home.

They walked inside and it was all different. Faith turned to Aaron as he closed the door and smiled. She felt all that uncertainty and dejection slip away from her as she watched him smile back.

"Make love to me, Aaron," she said simply.

He didn't need to be asked twice. Taking her hand, he led her to the bedroom.

This time, she knew she wouldn't wake up alone.

He kept his eyes on her as he slipped her jacket off. Slowly, he undid the buttons of her shirt dress and slid that down her arms, too.

"You're so beautiful," he murmured.

Leaning down towards her, he kissed her softly. The brush of his lips was a gentle promise of everything they'd left unsaid. Faith sighed gently as his fingers feathered up and down her arms, the light touch making her tremble. His hands moved over her rounded belly and made her moan.

He pulled her closer to him as he deepened the kiss, she felt him undo her bra and slip that off her. In a move so quick it made her gasp, she felt him sweep her up into his arms and carry her to the bed.

Faith watched as he got rid of his clothes quickly and saw that his hands weren't completely steady. That warmed her.

She smiled as she saw how beautiful he was. She didn't think she would ever get over how perfectly handsome he was.

He moved over her, covering her body with his and kissed her, long and deep, lips brushing, tongues meeting and dancing so softly and gently.

"Aaron…"

His name was a soft plea as she breathed it.

"I know," he whispered as he kissed her neck, his tongue leaving wet trails as he moved to the curve where he could feel her pulse beating madly.

Faith's breasts felt heavy as he kissed the slope of them. She watched as his pale hand made such a contrast with her dark skin, moving over her so softly. His fingertips moved over her breasts, but didn't touch her dark buds that strained towards him.

He kissed his way down her, his lips moving so close to her nipples but not touching them until Faith's breathing got harsh and ragged.

"Aaron, please…"

Finally, she felt his fingertips brushing against her nipples and she trembled. His tongue moved over them, first one and then the other, making her writhe against him. She found her hands on the back of his head, urging him to take more.

When his lips finally closed around her nipple and sucked, his teeth grazing it slightly, Faith cried out in pleasure. He pushed her breasts together and took both her nipples greedily into his mouth, sucking lightly, making her back arch as she gave him more, and more.

His hands moved down her body. Faith's legs fell apart as if of their own volition, needing him to touch her where she was so hot and wet, so desperately needy for him.

Aaron's mouth never left her breasts as his fingers moved over her crotch, touching her so delicately. He brushed his fingers over her panties, and the friction of that soft cloth against her wet heat was almost more than Faith could take. He pressed, touched, rubbed, and Faith squirmed as she felt her body respond with an intensity that shook her.

He slipped his hand underneath the fabric and Faith moaned her approval.

His lips became more insistent at her breasts as his fingers touched and probed, sliding between her lips and stroking her softly. She was so wet, so ready for him. He knew he could slide home, inside her, in one stroke and take her at that moment.

He knew she wanted him too.

"Aaron, please, I need you. I need you inside me, I need you to take me," moaned Faith.

When he raised his head from her breasts, she whimpered in protest. But the cool air on her wet breasts made her nipples even harder. His mouth moved down her body, trailing hot, wet, open-mouthed kisses that made her tremble.

She watched as he kissed her belly softly, before moving farther down. His tongue tickled the curves of her hips. She felt his lips press against her panties and wanted his tongue on her more than she had ever needed anything in her life.

"Aaron, please, I need you," she gasped.

Faith felt him draw her panties down, finally, and she spread her legs shamelessly, urging him to lick her, kiss her, tongue her to ecstasy. Her hips moved under his gaze, needing that last barrier gone. When he bunched it and threw it aside, Faith gloried in how he looked at her, how hungry he was for her.

She needed his mouth on her pussy. She needed to feel his cock filling her as he made love to her with a desperation that gratified her.

But he watched her, his gaze so intense that she felt it as potently as if he had touched her. Keeping his eyes on her wet, glistening pussy, he slid one finger along her slit, making her legs tense and tremble. He wanted to tease her until she needed him so much that she cried for him.

He spread her lips there and watched her get wetter still as he found the swollen nub of pleasure that cried out for his touch. He touched her there delicately, softly, until Faith's hips rose off the bed for more. He then drew little circles around it as Faith moaned and begged for more.

"Aaron please, touch me, please!"

"Shh, baby. I will. Let me watch you. I want to see all of you, see you as I pleasure you. I'll give you everything. I promise."

He was so hard that he didn't know how much longer he could hold on. But he wanted to watch Faith climax first.

Pushing down his own need, he pleasured her with his fingers, keeping her spread, watching as he touched and teased her, sliding his fingers inside her, curling them gently to make her gasp and cry out.

Finally, he moved closer and licked her, long and slow, again and again, until he felt her body begin to tense. His lips closed on her clit and sucked gently as his fingers slid deep inside her. Faith felt everything inside her coil and tense before she found that exquisite release shatter inside her and flood through her. She screamed his name as she came, her body shuddering over and over again.

Swiftly, Aaron moved over her. She was still trembling as he pushed his hard manhood deep inside the wet pulsing heat of her center. He held her as he finally let go and thrust, deep inside her, pulling out all the way before thrusting deep again.

He filled her and took his pleasure. Faith wrapped her arms and legs around him, urging him to take more. Desperate for more, Faith's hips pumped as she thrust up to meet him. She wanted him to fill her, stay inside her.

"You're so wet, Faith. You need me. Tell me that you need me," demanded Aaron.

"I need you, God, yes, please don't stop."

"Tell me what you need."

"I need your cock inside me. I missed having you inside me. I need you to fuck me like that, harder, please, Aaron fuck me harder!"

He gave her what she needed, driving into her harder, feeling her clutch at him as she felt everything rise again.

Her nails dug into his back as she felt herself rise to the crest of that wave of pleasure again. This time, she wanted him to tumble with her.

"Aaron, please, with me," she whispered as she kissed his neck.

"Faith," he groaned as he thrust deep inside her once again and let himself explode, spilling his seed within her, holding her to his heart.

Holding each other, tangled together, still joined, they fell asleep. For the first time in a week, both Aaron and Faith slept deeply and soundly, in each other's arms.

A few weeks later...

The doctor had given Faith the all clear, of course. She had got through her first trimester and everything was fine.

But Aaron looked so serious as they drove back home that Faith felt a bit uncertain. When they finally got home, he didn't get out of the car.

He turned to her.

"Faith, I need to ask you for something."

Faith smiled. She knew that she would give him anything.

"Okay," she agreed.

"I know we signed a contract. I'd like to tear it up."

Faith didn't feel any trepidation. She had known that he would ask. After all, a woman knows when a man is in love with her.

"I'd like that, too," she agreed.

Aaron looked surprised.

Faith chuckled.

"Oh, Aaron. I love you. I'm not going to step out of your life when I have your child. She's our child now. She's our daughter. We both know that."

Aaron looked slightly disgruntled.

"I never said that."

"But we both know that."

Slowly, he grinned.

"You're an infuriating woman. You didn't even let me come up with that myself."

Faith laughed.

"I'm infuriating, but I'm your woman. We both know that, too. And you're my man, Aaron."

As if she'd made the most commonplace of declarations, Faith got out of the car and walked to the door. Shaking his head, Aaron followed her.

It didn't matter that Faith was nothing like the woman he'd thought would be perfect for him. All that mattered was with her, he was happy. Without her, he was miserable.

She was right. She was his infuriating woman, and he was her man.

Martha's algorithm had done a lot more than it reckoned!

The end.

If you enjoyed this ebook and want me to keep writing more, please leave a review of it on the store where you bought it. By doing so you'll allow me more time to write these books for you as they'll get more exposure. So thank you. :)

Get Free Romance eBooks!

Hi there. As a special thank you for buying this book, for a limited time I want to send you some great ebooks completely **free of charge** directly to your email! You can get it by going to this page:

www.saucyromancebooks.com/physical

You can see a the cover of these books on the next page:

These ebooks are so exclusive you can't even buy them. When you download them I'll also send you updates when new books like this are available.

Again, that link is:

www.saucyromancebooks.com/physical

Now, if you enjoyed the book you just read, please leave a positive review of it where you bought it (e.g. Amazon). It'll help get it out there a lot more and mean I can continue writing these books for you. So thank you. :)

More Books By Ellie Etienne

If you enjoyed that, you'll love Her Billionaire Widower by Cher Etan (sample and description of what it's about below - search 'Her Billionaire Widower by Cher Etan' on Amazon to get it now).

Description:

Workaholic lawyer Angela needs a break.

Putting in time to make partner at her law firm, she finally decides it's time to take her daughter Nayda on a vacation. Their holiday soon takes an unexpected turn though when Nayda first makes friends with, then saves a boy from drowning at a Californian beach.

At the hospital, Angela meets the boy's dad David, a handsome billionaire and also a single parent.

Deciding to spend the week together due to their now-inseparable children, the two hit it off and end up starting a romantic relationship.

But will Angela, who still has work on her mind, be able to commit to the already-smitten David?

Want to read more? Then search 'Her Billionaire Widower Cher Etan' on Amazon to get it now.

Also available: Falling For His Surrogate's Sister by Erica A Davis (search 'Falling For His Surrogate's Sister Erica A Davis' on Amazon to get it now).

Description:

The Slade sisters haven't had the greatest time recently. Arlie suffered a miscarriage after a bad incident with her abusive ex-boyfriend, and Michelle hasn't been able to find any more teaching work since she got laid off.

So Michelle decides to become a surrogate for the rich, and is partnered up with eligible billionaire Matt Prentice; a man who wants a child more than anything.

Soon both parties decide it's best if Michelle moves in with him, but only if she can bring her sister Arlie for support.

However while Matt is working professionally with Michelle to have his baby, he quickly falls head over heels for her sister Arlie!

Will this new turn of events get too complicated for some?

Or will Arlie, Matt and Michelle all get the happy endings they deserve?

Want to read more? Then search 'Falling For His Surrogate's Sister Erica A Davis' on Amazon to get it now.

You can also see other related books by myself and other top romance authors at:

www.SaucyRomanceBooks.com/RomanceBooks

www.saucyromancebooks.com/romancebooks

CPSIA information can be obtained
at www.ICGtesting.com
Printed in the USA
LVOW13s2353080617

537488LV00009B/105/P